Tom Harrison, Surgeon

SELINA STANGER

To Susen with
love from
Selina

TOM HARRISON. SURGEON

DEDICATION

To the late great Phil Stanger, who kept the computer going for me against all odds.

TOM HARRISON. SURGEON

CONTENTS

TOM HARRISON. SURGEON

ACKNOWLEDGMENTS

Many thanks to Christine Richardson of Southsea for her diligent editing, and to artist Ruth Jones of Gorseinon for her brilliant book cover design.

I could not have written this book without the help and support of my family and friends, I appreciate their encouragement and patience. Especially Michael and Paula, Diane, Christine and Richard, for their interest and tolerance; Wendy Metcalfe for her inspirational teaching, who told me that writing a novel was 'doable'; Nicky, Frances, Gill, Di and Pam from the book group for their advice and support; and also Julia, Daphne, Sandie, Elisabeth, both Rosemarys, Peter and the Southsea WriteInvite group.

PEOPLE IN THE BOOK

Tom Harrison, apprentice surgeon
John Harrison, calico printer, Tom's father
Sarah Harrison, Tom's mother
Joe Harrison, farmer's boy, Tom's older brother
George Harrison, mill worker, Tom's younger brother
Robert Harrison, Tom's youngest brother
Elizabeth Harrison, Tom's younger sister
Mary Ann Harrison, Tom's youngest sister
Alice Harrison, married to Joe
Nipper, a boy related to Alice
Bridget Murphy later married to Robert
Mr.& Mrs. Murphy and Bridget's three brothers
William Jarvis, surgeon, Tom's mentor
Edward Brown, innkeeper,
Arthur Brown, Edward's son, friend of Tom

Martha Armstrong, farm gangmaster
Ben Armstrong, Martha's son
Benjie Armstrong, Ben's son
Charlie Armstrong, Ben's nephew
Fat Frank, Martha's foreman
Ox, Frank's brother
Caleb, young worker
Wiggy, older worker

Richard Graham, blacksmith
Nancy Graham, Richard's eldest daughter
Sally and Susan Graham, Richard's twin daughters
Jeannie Jordan, friend of Nancy
Mr. Watson, headmaster
Mrs. Hull, infant teacher
Adam, pupil teacher
Kit Dawson, apprentice blacksmith
Hamish (& family), Gretna Blacksmith
'Awkward' and 'Troublemaker' from Gretna

1 THE APPRENTICE

Tom had always wondered what was in the back room behind the apothecary shop, and Dr. Jarvis had told him to go in and have a look. The day before, Tom had been wading in the river, climbing trees and playing football with his friends. He had not planned ahead very much, but thought that he might like to work on a farm or in the quarry. Going to sea sounded exciting; the roar of the waves would be more fun than the clatter of mill machinery, the scratching of a clerk's pen or the scary silence of this little shop of horrors.

Tom opened the door and walked into the room very cautiously as he was not sure what he would find. The smell was overpowering; it must have been coming from some of the strange things in jars on the shelves. He got used to the gloom and could make out more of the hidden treasures, but wasn't sure whether that was a good thing.

Tom must have disturbed a large marble, and it rolled towards the front of a shelf: he caught it before it fell on the floor. Tom picked it up to look at it more closely; he nearly dropped it when it looked back at him.

"That glass eye belonged to poor old Sailor Jim," said Dr. William Jarvis cheerfully. "He fought Napoleon. A musket took Jim's eye out but I can't remember what happened to his leg."

Tom could just make out the shape of a wooden leg in the corner of the room. He put the marble back with a shudder; he was not quite so sure now that he would like to go to sea!

One of the jars looked just like a normal blue pottery kitchen jar, so Tom thought it would be safe to peep in. Thin black slug like creatures squirmed inside, and rushed towards freedom. He got the lid back on, but two of the beasties stayed on his hand and wouldn't let go. It seemed impossible, but they seemed to be slowly getting bigger, and biting. Tom was panicking and wondering what to do next.

William realized that his new apprentice had discovered the jar of leeches and was in a bit of trouble. Tom was tall and lanky for his age and awkward in his movements. He had big hands and feet and his sandy hair seemed to grow every which way.

"I see you have found my little pals," William said, expertly shaking a little salt on the offending leeches so they fell on the shelf and he could put them back into the jar. "Is that all of them? Leeches are difficult to come by, but I can always find a new apprentice". He sounded as if he was smiling as he said it.

"I think that is all, nothing is biting me now. What are leeches for?" Tom asked.

"If a patient's body humours are too hot or too wet, the patient has to be bled," explained William, looking over the top of his spectacles. "We put a few leeches on the patient's body to suck some blood; there is less damage than opening a vein. I will show you next time I do it".

"When a patient is ill, how do you know what is wrong?" Tom asked.

"Mostly it is straightforward. A farmer gets trampled by a horse, a labourer is crushed in the quarry, the midwives call us in, someone asks for some medicine or a tooth pulling." William said. "The physicians have book learning (like the vicar); they can work out what is wrong with a patient when it isn't obvious. Then we surgeons do the work to put things right. Physicians are gentlemen, like architects, and we are craftsmen like stonemasons."

The bell went in the shop. William said, "Just wait there a minute, have a look at the books if you like, you will probably be safe with those." Tom opened a book that was sticking out, taking care not to disturb the skeleton at the other end of the bookcase. Tom loved books; there were none at home and he had been through the Sunday School library twice. Was that really how bones were connected to the rest of the body? He looked at the skeleton again, trying to imagine it. Then William called him into the shop.

"We have to go up to the river this morning, as it looks like someone fell in and drowned last night." Tom gulped at hearing this. William continued, "I will have to take a look and report to the Coroner. It is best if you come with me, you will get into less trouble. You can watch and learn, carry my bag and make sure you do not gossip about any of our work. Keep your mouth shut this morning, except for when you are losing your breakfast."

***

Tom and William walked up towards the river, passing the green. There were a number of boys playing football and Tom noticed one or two of his friends amongst some other boys who did not look so friendly. He tried to hold his head up as he went past and tried to ignore laughing and calls of 'Tom Sawbones'. The laughter may not have been directed at him, but Tom felt that he stuck out like a sore thumb, following the surgeon and carrying the bag.

"What happened at the river last night?" asked Tom.

"Mr. Beattie asked some men from Martha Armstrong's gang to move timber from the river bank yesterday. He treated them to some whisky last night for their trouble, to bring a little joy into their lives. As the men were on their way back, one of them fell off the bridge into the river and the current took him." said William.

"Couldn't the others rescue him?" asked Tom.

"They couldn't find him; it was pitch black and they were befuddled due to the whisky. I am sure they did their best, but the current can be quite swift," answered William.

They arrived at the footbridge and could see where the unfortunate man had slipped. "You can't be clumsy in this world and get away with it," said William. Tom realized this little gem of wisdom was directed at him.

They found the man about fifty yards downstream, washed up on the shore. Tom had spent a lot of time playing, swimming, diving and fishing here, but it seemed a long time ago now. He knew the river claimed victims, but they were usually strangers, not local men. In spite of the sun sparkling on the surface, the river looked gloomy.

Tom stood by with the bag, watching William check the man carefully.

"What are you doing?"

"Firstly checking whether he is dead or just sleeping. Then I look for marks of violence or signs of foul play. The only injuries on him look as if he hit the roots and stones in the river. It appears that he just slipped on the bridge; they must have been staggering a bit, and probably singing and dancing. There are no signs that he was pushed, or that he jumped."

"Who is he?"

"Ben Armstrong, Martha's son, a widower with a boy of eleven. Ben's life must have been grim, but at least he died happy. I am off to Martha's to arrange for her gang to fetch the body. I want you to stay with Ben until I get back."

When William had gone, Tom moved upstream a little. He could see if anyone approached and watch over Ben without being too close. He was near the pool where he had watched his older brother tickle trout. Tom remembered the way his brother Joe had kept his hands still in the water until a fish swam nearly over the top, and then suddenly made a skilful grab. Joe had gone to learn farming with Uncle Isaac in Westmorland and Tom did not have Joe's patience or his deftness. Tom was about to give up, and his sleeves were very wet before a medium sized trout gave itself up. William was approaching, so Tom hid the fish in his cap under a bush and moved nearer to Ben. William had missed nothing and pointed out Martha's gang – three men and a very small boy carrying a gate to act as a bier.

They could only move very slowly with the burden, as the boy was struggling to keep up. William reclaimed his bag, and told Tom to take young Benjie Armstrong's corner. They still moved at a fairly sedate pace; Tom was bigger and stronger than Benjie, but not quite as competent as the others. Benjie followed the bier as befitted the chief mourner; when he looked up he had surprisingly blue eyes under his shock of dirty black hair. When the group passed the green, the boys did not call out. Tom thought he had gained a new respect by doing a man's job, but the boys were more likely to be a bit afraid of some of the men in Martha's gang.

Benjie took up his burden again as they approached the hovel where Martha and her gang lived, with its ramshackle collection of outbuildings. A small, dark, bad tempered woman came out to give orders to the men.

"What took you so long? Take him in and then get back to work and that includes you, Benjie. I expect all your work finished today, and none of your laziness."

The men hurried off. Turning to Tom and William, she said, "You can go back to work as well. And I am not paying you any money, so don't bother sending a bill!"

When they were out of earshot, Tom asked, "What will become of Benjie; will he go on the parish now his father is dead?"

"No, he would be better if he did, at least he would be apprenticed and learn a trade. Martha will make him take his father's place in her gang and work him far too hard like she does the others," said William. "Mind you, a little hard work does no harm. This afternoon I am making up medicines, and I want you to deliver them around the town – and no going fishing instead of working!"

***

Tom's last errand was a delivery to Mr. Graham, the blacksmith. Tom remembered sitting next to Nancy Graham at Sunday School. When she was younger she used to play out with Tom and his brothers but she was a bit above such things now. She was a pleasant looking girl, with warm brown hair and freckles, very much in command of herself.

"I see you have brought a bottle of jollop for my dad. He will be in a much better temper when his joints are not aching so much. So you are the new Sawbones apprentice; none of the others could stomach it for long. Dr. Jarvis usually tests his lads out for a week or two before the indentures are signed. I have heard a lot of scary stories. What is really in that back room of his?"

"Lots of books, more than I have ever seen before. And a few bits and pieces for his work. I will know a bit more soon because he told me to start cleaning the room out tomorrow." Tom talked as if the back room was full of surgeons' mysteries, to be kept from the general public if the medicines were to be effective.

"I heard there was to be a school here in Gorton, weekdays as well as Sundays. Do you know what is happening?" asked Tom.

"The Sunday School building is to be used for a day school, so mill owners and other important people are hiring schoolteachers. Your young brothers and sisters might go to school, even little Mary Ann. When my twin sisters go, I will be free to learn a trade, I will be a dressmaker or a milliner," said Nancy proudly.

"Why do you want a trade, when you are busy at home with your father and the girls? When the girls grow up, I will marry you and you can look after me."

"I want to earn my own bread; no man shall keep me. I would be a schoolmistress but I am not sure if I am bossy enough."

Tom had heard her ordering her sisters about, and thought she would make an excellent schoolmistress.

Tom arrived home with his fish; it looked a little small for seven of them but his mother said there were peas and beans to pick from the garden to make it go further. He dug some potatoes while his mother shelled the beans, and felt proud that he had helped to provide some of the family's meal.

After dinner Tom's father took Tom for a little walk.

"What did the surgeon teach you today, lad?"

"To keep my mouth shut and watch what I am doing,"

"Those are good lessons, lad, wherever life takes you. I didn't want all our family to depend on the cotton mills too much; people will always need farmers like Joe and surgeons like you. If we go ahead and sign the indentures, you won't be paid for the first two years of the four-year apprenticeship, and then you will have journeyman work for other surgeons for a year or two. Are you still hankering after going to sea?"

"I don't want to go to sea anymore. I am happy to be apprenticed to Dr. Jarvis, if he will have me."

2 THE TRAVELLER

Tom knocked on the blacksmith's kitchen door, trying not to drop the bottle in his hand and hoping that he had timed his errand correctly. When he was invited in, he was delighted to see that the fire was burning brightly, casting a warm glow over everyone. Even better that the kettle was boiling and Nancy was busy making toast.

Tom had always tried to put a finger on the difference between this kitchen and the one at the surgery. Both houses served as places of work, but the blacksmith's house seemed to be more of a home. The stone floor was always swept, whether it needed it or not. There were no cobwebs and everything was in its place. No books or papers graced the table. Perhaps it was the 'woman's touch' that made the difference.

"Good to see you, lad, I was waiting for that bottle of jollop," said Richard."

Please stay for tea and tell us about your travels. How was Penrith?" He was never happier than when holding court around the tea table, offering hospitality to all comers. The kitchen was cosy; the hob, fire irons, coalscuttle and toasting fork were in position and the dresser stood proudly against the wall, all the plates on display. The table, chairs and stool were in position and Nancy was setting another place for tea.

"Penrith was really good, a bit like Gorton but there is more farming and no big mills. The people were very friendly and I was quite sorry to leave." said Tom.

"Did you like it better than Hilltop?"

"Hilltop was really cold, and windy and bleak. But Joe was there and my uncle and they were really pleased to see me and get all the news. Hilltop doesn't have the same diseases as they do here, the wind must blow them all away. But a man can freeze to death when he goes out to look after the sheep, or he can lose fingers and toes to frostbite," Tom shivered, remembering. "It is lovely and warm here."

"Do some places really get cut off for weeks in the winter?"

"Quite often. Hilltop is made up of several little villages and they can be cut off from each other as well as from the outside world. Joe's village would have been left without a doctor if I hadn't gone over to see him just before the snow set in. There was no animal doctor and I had to help with the early lambs as well; I learned a lot there," said Tom. Nancy blushed.

"I must just tidy the yard before tea, you can tell me all about it then. But not too much detail on those fingers and toes, or the lambs."

"You can make yourself useful and do some extra toast, while I make the tea," said Nancy, handing Tom the toasting fork.

Tom didn't do very well as he was busy watching the children playing schools. Tom could not believe how much the little girls had grown in the two years since he had been away.

Nancy's sister Susan was pretending to be the teacher, and she had her twin Sally, the cat, and Tom's sister Mary Ann sitting in a little row. They each had their own slate and were solemnly reciting the alphabet; the cat was getting a bit fidgety because the girls had made it wear a pinafore.

Susan was getting more and more cross, and got out her ruler in case someone made a mistake. The cat broke ranks and sat a little distance away, washing itself as if it had nothing to do with the little girls. Susan stood up and the cat ran off, trailing its pinafore as the strings slowly unravelled.

"You haven't listened to a word I have said, have you?" asked Nancy.

"Sorry," said Tom, trying not to laugh." You've your own class now, at the school?"

"If you had been paying attention you would know that I've had my own class for the last year. I teach all the eight, nine and ten year olds, which is where the real work is done. Some of the older children go out to work in the mill in the afternoons, and of course the infants just sing and play all the time."

Susan tried to tell her that the infants had to work very hard on their letters and numbers, but Nancy ignored her and told the little girls to go and wash their hands, ready for tea.

"You are making a right pig's ear of that toast, Tom. I had better do the rest while you scrape the burnt bits off. Did you see any pretty girls in Penrith?"

"I didn't really notice. I suppose I must have done."

"Prettier than me?" asked Nancy. Tom hesitated, which was not what she wanted. "Careful with that scraping, don't make a mess."

"There was nobody like you, Nancy," said Tom, "You are still my girl."

"I heard that you went to see Jeannie the other day. She is a very pretty girl."

"I suppose so. I went to see her with my brother George and it looks as if he is quite smitten with her. Do you see much of Arthur these days?"

"He's helping his father with the ale house; I suppose we must call it an inn now they have all that coaching trade."

"He has very good prospects then."

"Yes but he was always a bit of an old woman. I could never take a man in an apron seriously. I suppose that toast will have to do – the black bits won't show under the bramble jelly."

Tom settled down to enjoy his meal, and looked forward to the time when Nancy was presiding over his own tea table. She would have to give up her job, and spend her time looking after him and supporting him in his important work. Tom thought it was the teaching that made Nancy a bit bossy; it must spoil a woman to have a class full of children following her orders, but that could soon be put right.

3 THE CITY

Nancy had heard that Tom was back from Carlisle, and came to visit him in the apothecary shop where Dr. Jarvis lived. Originally a house like all the others in the terrace, the front room had been turned into a shop. The large shop window held intriguing bottles of coloured liquid and lotions and potions to cure all ills. There were always remedies to ease joint pain, indigestion and colic but the rest depended on the season. Currently the cough mixtures were replacing summer medicines like calamine lotion, and it looked very much a work in progress.

The shop had a small dispensary behind screens that also served as a consulting room. It was out of sight of the queue of people in the shop but not out of earshot, but in a small town everyone knew what was going on anyway. Tom said that they always got extra customers if there was to be a tooth pulled or a boil lanced.

Nancy looked around her; the shop was familiar enough but she was relieved when William Jarvis suggested that he would mind the shop for a bit while she and Tom went through to the kitchen. The room was large, with a door leading to the narrow stairs to the bedrooms. There was an archway leading to a scullery that jutted into the small, enclosed garden, and a door leading to a room that started off as a study but got rapidly full of the things that no doctor could do without. Their charwoman would not go near the study as the skeleton gave her the creeps, and she fought a losing battle trying to clean the rest of the house.

The kitchen table was used for dining, writing, and for mixing medicines when the doctors wanted to keep the mystery about the ingredients. One or two specimens from jars in the murky study had been brought in for dissection. And it looked as if all these activities were in progress on the table at the same time so Nancy decided not to look too closely.

"Where have you been travelling to this time?" asked Nancy, as though she had not been asking Mary Ann and Jeannie about Tom's progress.

"The big city, Carlisle. It was so large, the rows of houses seemed to go on forever and I have never seen so many mills. There is a big castle in red stone and ladies and gentlemen that wear silk and satin instead of wool and cotton," said Tom.

"What are the ladies like? Are they very beautiful?"

"It is difficult to see under all those big hats and false curls."

"Did you go anywhere else?" asked Nancy. She was very envious and would have liked to work in strange new places.

"I went to Hilltop again; it is much better in the summer. The air is lovely and fresh and everybody looks well, so there was not as much for me to do. One of the children got badly sunburned, so we had to dip him in a churn of sour milk. He smelt for a day or two but it did the trick."

"I never heard of such a thing! Did it really work?"

"Like a charm, his parents could have lost him otherwise. The family had come from Manchester and were not used to all that sun and wind."

"Not much danger of sunburn here," said Nancy. She smiled as she thought of some of the children in her class who would benefit from being dipped in sour milk. "You forget that I went to Hilltop; we danced at Joe's wedding."

"It was lovely to dance with you; I know we haven't seen much of each other but I might be home for good after I have been to Edinburgh."

"People of our age are beginning to settle down and get married. Jeannie and George are walking out. I didn't know he was on a full man's wage."

"He isn't, but Jeannie will do dressmaking for some of her customers after she marries. Married women are not allowed to teach, but they can do dressmaking or work in the mill. I can't be sure yet whether I will be working here with Dr. Jarvis, so it might be a good idea to wait before we make any plans. Not everybody our age is settling down, Arthur is still single."

"I heard that he liked the butcher's daughter, I don't know what he sees in her."

"Crafty old Arthur! So he has got his feet under that table, has he?"

"Aren't you going to make me any tea, then?"

"Sorry, I forgot," said Tom apologetically. He went to the scullery and came back with an old kettle that was completely black down one side, put two spoonfuls of tea in it and put it on the hob. Nancy shuddered.

"Do you always make tea like that?" Haven't you got a teapot?"

"Somewhere," said Tom, "I'll go and look." He searched and finally came back from the study with a very dirty teapot. "It has had leeches in it; do you think I need to wash it out?"

"Tea from the kettle will be fine," said Nancy faintly." Don't bother with the teapot."

"I wish you would make up your mind. You are in luck today; we have some damson jam to go with the bread." He looked along a row of grubby jars, selected the most promising and dusted the cobwebs off it.

"Just butter, please," said Nancy as she watched him cut bread into thick uneven slices. She would make sure that Tom changed his ways when they got married.

4 THE JOURNEYMAN

Tom strode confidently into the back room behind the apothecary shop, and started to put down various bundles. He remembered his cautious entry into the shop as an apprentice, eight years earlier. The shop seemed smaller now, and not as terrifying. Now Tom was a journeyman on the verge of qualification as a surgeon.

"So how did you enjoy working in Edinburgh?" asked William.

"Not as much as Carlisle and Penrith and some of the smaller towns but I got the chance to go to some of the lectures with the new physicians. I have a few more books. Is there room for them here?" said Tom.

"As long as there are not too many. Were the lectures helpful?"

"I have a pretty good idea of what is inside people, so I know where to be careful when I am removing bullets and the like," said Tom as he started putting the larger books in the gaps on the shelves. "Not quite so much about how people work, but the professors are learning all the time; soon they will know everything and write more books."

"Did you go to Professor Munro's anatomy lectures?"

"Some," said Tom as he unpacked another set of books. "All the corpses he used were convicted murderers, sentenced to be hanged and dissected. Like being hung, drawn and quartered, I suppose, only not so painful. You could see some disease on the body, (not always much for the younger ones) and you didn't need to puzzle out the cause of death because it was always obvious – great big rope marks".

"Did you go to any of the other lectures? Careful, I think that shelf is full."

"Dr. Christison is an excellent speaker, but he didn't do quite so many anatomy lectures because he couldn't get enough corpses. He was entitled to the murder victims, but sometimes they had gone off a bit - not nice and fresh like the felons," said Tom cheerfully as he tried to find spaces for the remaining books. "I found his talks really useful. I will be able to make reports for the Coroner with a bit more confidence now. And Dr. Knox, I went to one or two of his."

"I heard they were very well attended; what were they like?"

"Even though there were sometimes five hundred of us, we could all see and hear quite well. We didn't ask where he got his corpses from, but I suppose you know all about that," said Tom as he forced the last book into place.

"We don't get much news here."

"Well, Dr. Knox always had a good supply of corpses, and we supposed that bodies had been donated to science – for the advance of knowledge," said Tom. "I didn't like to think that people had been robbing graves in the dead of night. Some of them had no signs of disease and not a mark on them, and someone recognized Daft Jamie and he would never have written a will. It turned out that Burke and Hare were murdering victims just to sell their bodies for anatomizing. Mrs. Hare kept a fleapit of a lodging house, so there was a steady supply of vagrants who would not be missed. I can tell you this, as a fellow medical man. Not the sort of thing I can talk about at home, as my mother would worry."

"Well what happened to Burke and Hare?"

"They got careless about witnesses, and a few of their victims were recognized as well. Hare turned King's evidence, and Burke was tried and hanged."

"Was he dissected?"

"Oh yes, "said Tom. "The professor gave souvenirs of his skin to all his friends. We did a bit of trade ourselves, to all the ghouls who came up from London. No bones, as everyone could see his skeleton hanging up. Acres of skin, mostly as wallets and purses – I am much better at stitching now."

"Was all the skin his?"

"Skin is skin. They couldn't tell the difference. Serves them right for coming to Edinburgh to buy it," said Tom as he started unpacking another box.

"You haven't brought any back, have you?" said William, stepping back quickly from the box Tom was unpacking.

"No, I sold all I had. Maybe I could get you some if you want," said Tom but one glance at William told him the effort would not be required. "I have brought a skull; my mother probably wouldn't want it at home. It might make a good paperweight on the desk here. It's cleanish."

"We could do with a paperweight. Is there anything else?"

"A few little jars that might not be welcome at home. And some notes; can I leave them in this corner until I find a bookbinder? They would be more use to me here," said Tom as he cleared a space.

"So you made a bit of extra money then."

"I made a little playing cards as well.' I was not so good at billiards. I was thinking of buying a horse with my ill-gotten gains."

"Now you are of age and have finished your training, you are a qualified practitioner. You are now a master surgeon instead of journeyman. Had you thought of buying into a practice?"

"I haven't got that sort of money."

"My practice has grown and I am looking for a partner. I thought 'better the devil you know than the devil you don't'. If you have any capital to put in, the practice could buy a second horse. If you agree, I will come and see you and your father, and we could talk terms. I think it may be a good idea to have a Tontine, if you both agree."

"That is amazing! I hadn't expected to be so lucky. Are you sure I am good enough?"

"I've had splendid reports from the other surgeons you worked with, in spite of your outside interests at Edinburgh," said William. "I am very sure".

"Thank you. I'll work hard and try to be worthy," said Tom "But what is a Tontine?"

"If one partner dies, the other inherits their share of the practice. I'm an old man."

"You're in your prime."

"I've no family and I would expect to go first in the normal course of events. But if you fell off your fine new horse and broke your neck, I wouldn't want your relatives to sell your half and put me out of business. The practice would pay for the funeral, of course – as fancy as you like," said William.

"That's a sobering thought," said Tom, "I will have to be careful; no racing."

"If you were a partner, you would be in a position to marry. Nancy Graham was asking when you were coming back."

William's clear grey eyes missed nothing as he peered at Tom over the top of his spectacles. Tom felt as if he was a naughty boy again, explaining away his misdeeds.

"Yes, I suppose so."

"You don't seem keen."

"Yes, I am but…. I would like to get settled first. Get used to my new status, see my friends, show off the horse, that kind of thing," said Tom as he rounded up his few remaining bundles. "Anyway, I still don't think of you as an old man; you might marry."

"I am too set in my ways now. I will never marry."

William was gaunt and frail, his stoop was more pronounced and his hair was completely white even though he couldn't have been more than fifty. He won't be quite so tired when we are sharing the work, thought Tom.

Tom's father, John, seemed much more vigorous than William, even though he was the same age. John was tall and spare, an older version of Tom. It is funny how most of us resemble father, Tom thought. Most of us have his slow, careful way of speaking and acting, and his preference for a quiet life, but Joe and Robert resembled their mother Sarah in looks, shorter with a darker complexion. The youngest child, Mary Ann, resembled Sarah in her manner. They were both very active, always bustling about, and taking an interest in everything.

Tom gave his father a very edited version of the events in Edinburgh and told him about William's offer, explaining that he would be investing his own money and would not need a contribution from his parents. He did not elaborate on how he had managed to save money.

John was a little unclear on the difference between a partner in a practice and any other qualified worker, but was pleased that Tom's future was settled. He chuckled over some of the Edinburgh stories.

"I know what you young fellows get up to, but we won't tell your mother. There is only Elizabeth and Mary Ann at home with us now. Joe is well set up at Hilltop; he is a master brewer now and helps to run the inn; they get a lot of travellers stranded there in the winter. Young Robert went off to be a miner and George is going to get married soon; they are reading the banns for the first time on Sunday," said John.

"Nancy said that he was courting," said Tom.

"I have been walking out with Jeannie Jordan since Michaelmas," said Tom's younger brother George, who had just come into the garden and was pleased to see Tom again. "You should try and keep up with the news. I have finished my apprenticeship as a Calico Printer but I won't be on man's wages until I am twenty-one.

"I think I can remember Jeannie from school."

"Jeannie is a dressmaker now, and a friend of Nancy Graham. Nancy was asking when you were coming back; she is hoping to see you in church on Sunday. Jeannie and I usually go for a walk afterwards."

"I will be there," said Tom.

"Your mother and I would like to see you married and settled down now you have finished gallivanting. Even young Robert is courting, over in Gateshead," said John.

"I don't know, I am much too young, I hadn't really thought about it."

"Your mother and I were married with two babies by the time we were your age. Nancy is a good steady girl, a schoolmistress and managing her father's household as well. You could do a lot worse."

"She rules those school children with a rod of iron, according to Mary Ann. Mr. Watson is such a wet hen that he sends his naughty boys to Nancy for the cane," said George.

"Is that normally what happens in schools these days?" asked Tom. "I am a bit out of touch."

"Normally the headmaster would do the caning but Nancy is Nancy," said George "She is very good at it."

Tom shuddered. "I may not be able to come on Sunday, there is the possibility that we could get called out to a patient. But I will be there if I can." He decided that it might be a good idea to stay at the shop for a while, to make it easier for William. Mrs. Hodgson was due to have her fourth and the midwives might call the doctors in if they thought it was necessary. The mothers and midwives usually preferred the doctors not to attend but Tom felt that they might be needed.

***

The message from the Hodgsons came too late and William Jarvis found each childbirth more and more difficult. It did not seem to faze Tom, but then he was a newly qualified surgeon and still learning. It took William back to the day when his mother died giving birth to his brother, all those years ago. The darkened room, the heat, the hushed voices, the herbs that the midwives used, nothing had changed in forty years.

 "I'm sorry, but there is nothing more we can do," said Tom.

"Is there no hope at all?" asked Mr. Hodgson.

"She is fading fast, it is time for you and your daughters to say your goodbyes," said Tom.

William froze, watching the scene as if through a window. The sadness was not as overpowering now, but his sense of failure made everything worse. This was the nineteenth century after all, and women should not be dying like this. All those years of work and study and there was still nothing that he could do.

William was still very unsteady as they walked back to the shop. Tom forgot all about going to church. He unexpectedly realized that his parent's generation might not have all the answers anymore.

***

At the shop, Tom and William had a comforting drop of brandy, and both felt a bit better.

 "England and the Empire are prospering, we have just fought a war to end all wars, but country doctors like me do not know enough to help the patients. Women should be living out their allotted span of fifty years, not dying in childbirth," said William.

"All the best doctors in London couldn't help King George's daughter and her baby," said Tom. This was not the right thing to say. William's mind went off on a tangent.

"King Billy has no children. There is only little princess Victoria between the wicked Duke of Cumberland and the throne; what will become of us if she dies like her cousin?" asked William.

"Then we will be a republic like France, and take over the world!" said Tom. "I could go to sea and be a ship's surgeon. But I think princess Victoria will survive."

It was only afterwards that Tom remembered that he had missed seeing Nancy but it couldn't be helped. Maybe he would call during the week. He was a professional man now, and William and the patients must come first.

5 THE SCHOOLMISTRESS

Nancy Graham sat at the back of the church with her father, Richard, and her twin sisters, Sally and Susan. Richard would have preferred to sit nearer the front so that he could hear the sermon but Nancy and her sisters wanted to be able to see everybody without turning round. As a schoolmistress, Nancy was used to having her own way, Richard just wanted a quiet life.

Nancy could see her friend, Jeannie Jordan, sitting with her family. Jeannie was looking around for the Harrisons to arrive. Nancy thought that Jeannie was making a spectacle of herself; dressmakers like Jeannie were known to be a bit frivolous but schoolteachers were expected to show some decorum. The Harrisons finally walked in, father John, mother Sarah, and the two girls. Mary Ann smiled at Sally and Susan; Elizabeth still seemed to be coughing a bit. George arrived, but there was no sign of Tom. Nancy knew that Tom had arrived back from his travels. She had heard that he was now a master surgeon; it seemed funny to think of her former playmate as a grown man with an important job. Perhaps he was needed somewhere else (that sounded funny too) and would arrive later; he had promised to be there.

Nancy watched Jeannie blush as George went past, even though they had been courting for some time. Nancy wished she were 'walking out' with Tom; at twenty-one she was getting to be an old maid. In her prominent position as schoolmistress, she would be a figure of fun for the whole town if she were left on the shelf. To relieve her feelings, Nancy glared at Sally for fidgeting.

Lost in thought, Nancy did not notice much of the church service, but she heard the marriage banns being called for George and Jeannie. Surely Tom would have wanted to listen to George's banns!

After the service, many of the people were standing in groups in the warm sunshine. Nancy walked over to Jeannie and George, but Susan followed her.

"I hear that Tom is back; I thought he would have been here today."

Susan giggled, and Nancy glared at her.

"Why don't you and Sally go and see Mary Ann," said Nancy hopefully, but Sally and Mary Ann had already arrived; they did not want to miss anything.

"Tom was hoping to come," said George, "but he has responsibilities now. He thought he might be called out to a patient. Sometimes men need patching up if there are fights on Saturday night."

Nancy was angry rather than disappointed; in her world people did what she expected. If there had been a fight, she would have heard her sisters discussing it; they always seemed to hear news before anybody else. Nancy thought that Tom should organize his working life better; when they were married, she would see to it. Nancy never let her work interfere with her Sundays, and neither should anybody else.

"George and I are going for a walk," said Jeannie. "You are welcome to come with us if you like."

Nancy declined with thanks and George and Jeannie went on their way. Susan giggled again and Nancy felt like slapping her. Nancy's father and sisters noticed her grumpiness and kept out of her way for the rest of the day.

***

Nancy had cooled off by the time Tom came to see her a few days later. He was still tall and lanky, but he had filled out and was not so awkward looking. His smile was still the same, but he looked tired.

"I thought you would have come to hear George and Jeannie's banns read on Sunday." said Nancy.

"We were called out to a patient in the early hours. Then Dr. Jarvis was taken poorly and I had to take him home and make sure that he was all right. I have been rushed off my feet ever since. That's why I'm here now," said Tom.

Nancy had hoped for a social visit, but tried to hide her disappointment as best she could.

"You want me to mind your shop or carry messages? I'll have you know that I have a very important job here as schoolmistress; my work is just as important as yours. When I am busy I get my pupils to do work for me; you should organize yourself better."

Tom ignored the outburst. Some of the townspeople still saw him as Dr. Jarvis's apprentice, but once he got his horse his real status would be more obvious.

"Dr. Jarvis and I are looking for an apprentice to start right away. I thought you might know of a suitable lad in your school."

"I'll consult Mr. Watson. "Perhaps you'd like to come to the school on

Friday morning and see some of the boys."

***

On Friday morning Nancy collected some of the exercise books for inspection, so the older boys knew that something was going on. It was Friday afternoon before William and Tom arrived at the school, which did not suit Nancy at all. She had been hoping to impress Tom with the way she taught the children and made them behave, and show the quality of their work under her tuition. Instead she was taking a sewing class, which anyone could do.

The younger girls were making calico bags to put their books in. At each stage they took their work to be inspected; sometimes it had to be unpicked and started again - some of the bags were looking a little grubby by now. Other girls had progressed to making calico aprons, and samplers. The real experts were adding embroidery to an ancient tablecloth. Nobody could remember who started the tablecloth; the work had been on the go for years and looked like it. There was a rumour that it got unpicked overnight so that it was never finished.

Some of the girls were not keen on sewing and discovered that if they couldn't find their needle, it took all lesson to find another one and file all the rust off it. Nancy was on to their little game; she set the tablecloth girls to take turns to read to the class while she conducted the needle hunt personally. She got her ruler from her desk and put it in a prominent position, ready for little knuckles if necessary. Three of the girls miraculously found serviceable needles and started working very diligently. The other two girls speeded up their search, their eyes brimming with tears. Nancy was at the back of the class rummaging through the sewing drawer, Mary Ann was in the teacher's chair reading from the Psalms, when William and Tom came in. They had been to see Mr. Watson first; another blow to her pride.

Nancy told Mary Ann to continue reading, while the visitors consulted her in Mr. Watson's office. Any class member who talked or got out of their chair must confess afterwards and be punished accordingly. This trick had always worked in the past.

Mr. Watson was an elderly man who looked tired and harassed. He suggested dismissing the children early so that there would be less gossip. Nancy thought that he didn't want to leave his class to their own devices in the garden where there were sticks and stones to play with.

"All the older boys' school work looks up to standard," said William, "and the boy who was mending the bean poles looked very competent."

"He's the carpenter's son, and expected to start work straight away," said Mr. Watson.

"There were four steady lads digging potatoes," said William. "Would any of them be suitable as a surgeon's apprentice?"

"They're due to start working in the mill," said Mr. Watson. "Their families need the extra money; none of them are in a position to be an apprentice."

"And the boy teaching the youngsters which beans were ready for picking?" asked Tom, thinking how lucky he had been to have his opportunity.

"Adam is an excellent worker," said Nancy.

"But we really need him ourselves next year, we need a pupil teacher now the school is getting bigger," said Mr. Watson. "Some of the boys are a bit unruly."

Nancy thought that the boys would not be unruly if Mr. Watson made more effort.

"Were those the boys picking the peas and raspberries?" asked William. "They seemed to be eating most of them."

"No, those boys are only ten and eleven," said Mr. Watson.

"Some of them are quite promising," said Nancy "but they are too young to be apprenticed."

"There were some lads scuffling and larking about, and teasing the little ones," said Tom. "Are those the twelve year olds?"

"Unfortunately, yes," said Mr. Watson. "But some of them may improve in a few months."

Nancy thought that they would improve straight away if she had a hand in it, but she was stuck with the sewing class on Friday afternoons.

"I think we will leave it for now," said William, "but I may come back to you in a few months if we can't find a suitable lad in a neighbouring parish. Your girls looked very well behaved, but our patients would never accept a woman surgeon."

"A woman would leave to marry and waste all the training," said Tom. He didn't fancy working with someone like Mary Ann.

"And they gossip," said Mr. Watson.

Nancy felt that they were being unfair, but there was nothing she could say. The girls would go into service, or the mill. Some of the lucky ones might become dressmakers or milliners. All that sewing would come in useful.

***

Tom walked Nancy home, but she was still bristling about the way her girls had been regarded.

"I thought that our Elizabeth was to be your next pupil teacher," said Tom, "she seemed to be very keen."

"She probably would have been, but her attendance hasn't been very good recently," said Nancy.

"You can't hold that against her," said Tom." My mam said she only has a bit of a cough."

"We need someone reliable. She has been very hit and miss this last year," said Nancy.

"Mam said that she would be right as rain soon, and there was nothing to worry about," said Tom. "It's very unfair that she has missed her chance." But he hadn't seen anything of his sister Elizabeth since he got back. Perhaps he would talk to his mother and see if he and William could help.

There was a distinctly cool atmosphere between Tom and Nancy when he reached her door, and she did not invite him in. Instead she went to see her father, who was in his workshop, examining a horse's shoes.

"You're home early today," said Richard, "did school finish early?"

"We let the children out a little bit early; the surgeons came looking for a new apprentice," said Nancy "but we had no-one suitable. They weren't pleased because they wanted one straightaway. They should give us more warning, instead of expecting us to produce a bright well behaved lad yesterday." She noticed that her father had a man with him, soothing a horse.

"You remember Benjie Armstrong, "said her father. "He's working at the stables at the moment."

Benjie looked up, and Nancy noticed that he had bright blue eyes under all that black hair. He smiled and his face seemed to light up.

"Pleased to meet you, Miss Graham," said Benjie in a surprisingly deep, melodious voice. Nancy felt a distinct tingle go through her body when she shook hands with him. She had felt nothing when she shook hands with Tom.

6 THE STABLE LAD

Benjie led the horse back to the stables and settled it down again. He always enjoyed visiting the blacksmith, a giant of a man who always had time for Benjie. Richard Graham was a lucky man with his cosy home and his three daughters to look after him. The girls were lovely, and seemed to be gentle like their father.

He thought about his own home with his grandmother, Martha Armstrong, or Ma Armstrong as she was called. She made sure that all her gang of labourers worked very hard, and that included him. They were all afraid of her, as she was likely to beat them for the least mistake. Usually her foreman, Fat Frank, did the beating and that was even worse.

Often her workers were hired out to other employers, but they never saw any of the money. Benjie was working as an ostler for Edward Brown, the landlord of the Queen's Arms, and life was much more comfortable, even if he had to sleep in the hayloft. The horses were much better company than Ma and Frank. He only saw Ma when she came into the town for her laudanum, gin and tobacco on Thursdays, and then he made sure he kept out of her way. With a bit of luck, Ma might forget all about him.

Benjie would have loved to stay on at the stables, but Mr. Brown said he needed to write and reckon a little better first. Benjie felt that he could remember what to charge the customers, and add it all up; he just didn't see why he had to write it all down. Miss Graham had said that she could help Benjie improve his writing; she would have a little spare time when the school finished for the holidays. He was really looking forward to spending more time with the wonderful Miss Graham. Benjie had a nagging worry about his young cousin as he set off on his errand to Dr. Jarvis.

"Mr. Brown said that he had one or two horses you might like to look at, Dr. Jarvis, Dr. Tom." said Benjie "I could show you them now if you like."

"This gelding would be ideal for a man of your height," said Benjie to Tom when they got to the stables. Benjie thought that Tom had not changed a great deal since he saw him last, except for getting even taller and filling out a little. Benjie was still small for his age, strong and wiry; he would never be as tall as Tom.

"Dobbin has a lovely nature; try him if you like." Benjie had a soft spot for Dobbin.

"Dobbin looks a bit like an old man's horse," said Tom after a sedate walk around the yard. "How fast can he go?"

"He's very reliable," said Benjie. "Old Barty used to take him to the ale house, and he knew his own place in the yard and never needed to be tethered. At the end of the evening Dobbin took Barty home, he knew the way, even when Barty had forgotten. That's why he walks so carefully; it was part of his job. Barty never needed to go home in the wheelbarrow, no matter what state he was in."

"Not the sort of horse I could race," said Tom. "How about this wonderful black stallion?"

"Have a go on Madman if you like," said Benjie, doubtfully.

"He's fine," said Tom, "he will just take a bit of getting used to." Tom did not feel quite so secure this time. He had ridden donkeys when he was younger, and William's slow plodder, but Madman was very different. Tom came off rather quicker than he had intended. It took him a while to untangle his foot from the stirrup.

"That's a real gentleman's horse," said William, smiling for the first time in days.

"What he means is, Madman is fine for a gentleman to show off to his friends. If you have a job of work to do, it makes it easier if the horse isn't trying to bite people or chase the mares," said Benjie. "Some more horses have just arrived; I can ask Mr. Brown to let you have first pick."

"Something with a bit of dignity, please. No piebalds or mares," said Tom. William smiled again.

"There's a fine grey gelding, younger than Dobbin. He used to belong to a squire's son and has taken part in one or two races. When the lad came into his father's money he bought himself a hunter, and sold this horse to us. You could name the horse yourself," said Benjie.

"A pale horse seems appropriate," said William.

"I'll call him Thunderbolt," said Tom. William seemed to be hiding his face in his handkerchief.

"I will call and see you next week when he has been checked over. I'm sure Thunderbolt will suit," said Benjie trying not to look at William. William had turned away from Tom by this time; his shoulders were shaking.

"Er ... are you still looking for an apprentice?" asked Benjie.

"Do you know of one?" asked William. "He would have to be bright, hardworking, well behaved and at least twelve years old."

"My cousin Charlie is twelve," said Benjie.

"Did we see him at the school?" asked Tom.

"He has been at the poorhouse for the last six months. When Charlie's parents died, he used to fend for himself. He did bits of work, ran errands for people and did a bit of fishing and rabbiting. He was fine until the farmer needed the cottage for a family and turfed him out. Charlie didn't want to work for our grandmother so he went to the poorhouse, and gran does not know he is living so near to us. When Charlie is thirteen he will either have to break stones with the poorhouse men, or work for the farm labouring gang. And gran might send him to the quarry or somewhere even worse," said Benjie.

"We can't let that happen," said William. "Has Charlie had much schooling?"

"He used to go regularly until he was ten, but then there were no pennies for the schooling. I think there are classes at the poorhouse," said Benjie.

"Charlie sounds as if he could do the job. If he has the basics of the three Rs we could send him to school in the mornings and pay for it ourselves," said William "We'll go to the poorhouse tomorrow."

"Er… might be better to go tonight. You would look as if you were going to the infirmary. If you want Charlie as an apprentice, it might be best to get the papers signed before gran finds out," said Benjie.

"Is it that important to be sneaky?" asked Tom.

"Yes, it is. And please can we keep it quiet that I told you about him; the Graham twins are terrible gossips. And, begging your pardon, Dr. Tom, your younger sister spends a lot of time with them," said Benjie.

***

Half an hour later, Benjie had unwelcome visitors.

"So there you are, all nice and comfortable," said Ma Armstrong.

Fat Frank didn't say anything, he just loomed. He was twice Benjie's size and four times as nasty.

"Have you seen anything of your cousin Charlie?" asked Ma Armstrong.

"Isn't he at the cottage?" asked Benjie.

"There's a new family there now," she said.

"That's right," said Fat Frank.

"Maybe he joined a fairground or something, or went to sea," said Benjie.

"I think that is very unlikely," she said. "He is more likely to be in a parish poorhouse somewhere. Can you remember which parish he was born in?"

"I think it was over Wetherall way," said Benjie, which would send them miles in the wrong direction.

"I will find him," she said. "Now he is old enough to work. I am his legal guardian so they will have to hand him over. I am your legal guardian, remember, until you are twenty-one. If I find that you have been lying,

Frank here will come and have a word with you. And you can forget all about your nice cosy job in these stables; I have been asked for more workers for the quarry."

As Benjie watched them go down the road, he hoped that the doctors would get to Charlie first. Benjie was nineteen and would take his chance, but Charlie was only twelve.

***

Later that night, Benjie wondered whether Charlie was all right. Then he comforted himself with happy thoughts about Miss Graham, how pretty she looked and how nice she was to him. He was sure she was a kind teacher, and the children in her class obeyed her because they loved her. He hoped he would be able to improve his writing and sums before gran and Frank caught up with him again.

7 THE NEW APPRENTICE

William was tired, but insisted that they should both visit the poorhouse straight away. The outside looked welcoming, with cheerful whitewashed walls, but the inside of the building seemed very bleak. Tom had seen the infirmary, but had realized there must be dormitories, workshops, kitchens and a refectory somewhere. There was a small amount of comfort in the Master's office, where they were waiting. Tom looked around; it seemed a world away from the bustle of the town.

"It's a dismal place," said Tom.

"It must be hard for older people who have worked all their lives and have nothing to show for it. If they have no money, and no family to look after them, they have to swallow their pride and ask to live here. They know that there is no going back. Some of the elderly just give up and die quickly to get it all over with," said William.

"What about the younger ones?"

"They have some hope of getting proper work, but the life here is very hard."

"Good evening, Dr. Jarvis, Dr. Tom. I am very surprised to see you both here. I didn't send for you, as all our people are sound in wind and limb at the moment. The Coroner hasn't sent you to check up on us again, has he? I wish he would leave us alone; we do the best we can with the money we have," said the Master.

"We are looking for an apprentice to start straight away," said Tom.

"We were going to have to look outside the parish, but thought we might come and see you first," said William. "Have you any lads of thirteen, or possibly twelve?"

"We have two twelve year olds, both very well behaved, and quite cheerful, considering. Kit Dawson is a big strong lad; Charlie Armstrong is small, but quite quick on the uptake," said the Master. He thought about one or two recent incidents involving Charlie but decided not to mention them.

"Can we have a look at their school work?" asked William. The Master rang a bell, and the books were brought in with a flurry of activity.

"Kit couldn't read or write at all when he came in, but he can sign his name now. Charlie can read very well, and reckon in his head, but he doesn't like writing very much," said the Master, trying to find a page without too many blots. "Neither of them will be up to the standard of the school; we can only give them a few lessons sometimes in the mornings."

"I think Charlie might do; can we see him now?"

"He will be in our tailor's shop. I will take you to him."

"It will be useful if he has learnt to stitch." said William

***

In the tailor's shop, a row of little old men sat cross-legged on a large table. One of them seemed to be whistling under his breath, but the Master looked sternly at him and he stopped. The offending whistler turned out to be a small boy with merry blue eyes and a grin that had not faded after six months in the poorhouse.

"Come with me to my office, Charlie."

"I haven't done anything, sir, honest," said Charlie, getting up while trying to hide the fact that he had been unpicking some of his work.

Charlie stood in the office, twisting his cap in his hands.

"These gentlemen are looking for a new surgeon's apprentice," said the Master.

"We want him to start right away," said William.

"Will I learn to chop off arms and legs, and cut up dead bodies?" asked Charlie.

"Not for many years, "said Tom. "You have many other things to learn first like running errands, cleaning the shop and looking after two bachelors. The more interesting bits will come later."

"You will need to practice your stitching, "said William. "And you need some more schooling so that you can study our books, and lots more writing practice."

"Miss Graham will sort you out there," said Tom cheerfully.

"I'm not sure that I want to go…" said Charlie, but the Master looked at him and he stopped.

"You don't realize how lucky you are."

"But what about my supper?" asked Charlie "I just finished my bread and water punishment and I've been looking forward to my supper all day."

"We haven't had our supper yet," said Tom. "I expect you are tired of bread but we have cheese, onions and some small beer. I think we have damsons as well."

"Damsons!" said Charlie.

"Everyone has his price," said William, sinking down onto a chair.

"I'll have to look up the rules for pauper apprentices; it is a long time since the last one," said the Master, rummaging through some papers. "Here we are. You take control of him until he is twenty-one; you are now his legal guardians providing food, clothes and somewhere to sleep."

"We have a truckle bed somewhere," said Tom.

"Let's get these papers signed," said the Master.

"We can lodge them with the authorities on Monday," said William.

"Here are the clothes you came in with, Charlie. You can't go out in poorhouse clothes, we will need them for someone else," said the Master.

"You must behave now you are an apprentice," said Tom. "No ale houses, or gambling. You must work very hard, and not gossip or get into trouble. Otherwise you will be punished."

"No ale houses or gambling ever?" asked Charlie, pausing as he got changed.

"Until you are twenty-one," said William.

It still seemed a long time to Charlie. He had another worry on his mind.

"Will you beat me?" asked Charlie.

"Not as hard as the Master does," said William," I am an old man, after all. Dr. Tom here would probably miss half the time."

"Miss Graham will be a different matter," said Tom.

"Get along with you, Charlie, before they find someone more deserving," said the Master. "If you work hard and qualify, you could do very well."

William felt very tired as they walked home, and rather regretted that they had not bought Dobbin when they were at the stables, he would have been very useful.

***

"So you have decided to join us in church at last, Thomas," said Sarah Harrison. "I thought you would have been living back home by now, instead of at that shop."

"Dr. Jarvis isn't very well at the moment, so I am doing all the visits so that he can get some rest. This means that I will need to live at the shop for a while so that people can find me," said Tom.

William had been just about to introduce Charlie to the little room behind the shop. Tom would have liked to stay and watch. However, he decided to come and look for his family at church before they came looking for him.

"Will you be coming for your dinner and tea today, Thomas?"

"I'll be able to come for dinner, but need to be back this afternoon in case I get called out."

They moved into church at that point, and Tom was glad of the enforced silence. His mind was in turmoil, with several worries. William was still looking tired, but insisted on a normal workload so the schedules needed skilful handling.

Charlie had strict instructions to fetch Tom if he was needed, but he hoped it would not be necessary during the morning. Tom didn't want it to be generally known that they had a new apprentice before the papers were lodged with the authorities the next day. Although the poorhouse Master was Charlie's guardian until the papers were lodged, Ma Armstrong was his next of kin so they had to be careful for a day or two.

Tom's other worry was Elizabeth. Nancy said she had missed a lot of school, and Elizabeth seemed to be much thinner than he remembered. She was coughing, but seemed as bright and cheerful as ever. He had seen a lot of consumption in the town, mainly people who worked in the mills; all that cotton dust would make anybody cough.

After church, Tom disentangled himself from his family and walked over towards Nancy who was standing with her father and sisters. Nancy looked quite different from last time he saw her; in her Sunday best she seemed almost a stranger, but when she spoke to him about his visit to the school, she was the Nancy that he remembered.

Tom and Nancy set off on their walk; Sally, Susan and Mary Ann followed them at a distance, trying to remain within earshot. Tom didn't want to discuss the school visit on Friday. Nancy would have liked to know whether he would choose a local boy but Tom said that nothing had been decided yet. He didn't want to talk about George's wedding; marriages were a long way from his mind. Instead Tom talked about his new horse and did not notice Nancy's bored silence.

John and Sarah Harrison cornered Tom before dinner with more questions. "I hear that you went to the school looking for a new apprentice," said John.

"Nothing is decided yet, none of the local lads are suitable at the moment," said Tom.

"Would you look outside the parish for an apprentice?"

"It would mean that the lad could live in the shop, fetch and carry for William and come for me when I am needed. It might make life easier."

"You could live at home, like you used to. Until your marriage, that is," said Sarah.

"I suppose so."

"You and Nancy would be a very good match."

"I am not in a position to marry just yet. William and the practice are taking up a lot of my time. It would not be fair on Nancy."

"But the practice is thriving," said John.

"William is not well at the moment; people might not want a clumsy great oaf like me looking after them. We might lose a few customers, then I would not be in a position to set up house."

"Surely not," said Sarah.

"Elizabeth seems a lot thinner, and is coughing more. Maybe we could help," said Tom, changing the subject.

"Old Dr. Pickersgill said that there was nothing wrong, only a cough," said Sarah.

"You see what I mean, customers prefer the older doctors."

"You are her brother. She has her modesty, we can't ask you what is wrong with her," said Sarah.

"Would you let William see her then? He is the best doctor in the town, much better than Dr. Pickersgill, Please, just to humour me."

"I thought he was too tired to visit anyone," said John.

"He would come out for Elizabeth. I will just mind the shop; it is all I am fit for."

"Oh, go on with you," said Sarah, but it was decided that William should visit Elizabeth.

***

Back at the shop, Tom explained the problem.

"Town dwellers and textile mill workers seem particularly prone to consumption; there is never so much in the country," said William, "What do the gentry in Edinburgh do?"

"Some of them go to their country houses where there is lots of fresh air. The really wealthy ones go to Switzerland."

"You have a brother living in Westmorland, I believe."

"That's right, right on the top of the hills," said Tom. "If there is the slightest doubt about Elizabeth she should not work at the mill for a while, if ever. See if you can persuade my parents to let her visit Joe and Alice in Hilltop; they will be glad of her help with another baby on the way."

"I'll see what I can do," said William. "I will call in after I have lodged Charlie's papers tomorrow."

"Where's Charlie," asked Tom, looking around.

"Picking damsons from the tree," said William, who seemed to have brightened up after Charlie's arrival." He has done his work, and it seemed a shame to keep him indoors."

"I hope no one saw him," said Tom. "I will stop worrying after tomorrow."

8 THE TUTOR

On her way home from school Nancy thought about her talk with Tom on Sunday, which she felt was very unsatisfactory. He hadn't mentioned marriage, and she hadn't liked to bring the subject up herself. All Tom had talked about was his horse; he was like a child with a new toy.

Tom had been very vague about the new surgeon's apprentice. She knew that Mr. Watson's eldest boys were not available, but she was sure that one of the twelve year olds would improve next year. But it looked as if the surgeons had found someone from outside the parish; Sally said that a boy had been seen climbing the tree in their yard on Sunday. Why did Tom not tell her on Sunday? Didn't he trust her? Why didn't he want her to know?

Nancy felt that if she taught the oldest children instead of the mid age range there would have been no problem. Her lads worked hard and behaved well, but would not be old enough for at least a year. If Nancy and Mr. Watson exchanged classes, she could sort those naughty boys very quickly. But Mr. Watson was the headmaster and the headmaster always taught the top class. Old Mrs. Hull always taught the infants; she would have preferred to teach older children but didn't trust Nancy with the infants – Mrs. Hull said there would be too many tears and wet drawers if Nancy taught the little ones. Nancy thought that the infants spent too much time singing, and had a lot of work to make up when they became juniors.

All very unsatisfactory, she thought; if Tom had talked to her, she could have sorted something out. People would think that the children from the school were not fit to employ, and would see it as being partially her fault when it wasn't. In the past Tom had always anticipated her wishes, and fallen in with what she wanted. Now he was almost a stranger, and didn't treat her as an equal anymore. Secretly she would like to have been treated as his superior. Tom still needed a lot of guidance. She also felt that Dr. Jarvis looked like a bit of a broken reed these days, unable to supply the common sense that Tom needed.

Nancy thought about Benjie; he always gave her the respect she deserved. Yes, Miss Graham; no, Miss Graham; certainly, Miss Graham – that was how the world should be. She was looking forward to Benjie's visit the next day, and to helping him with his writing and arithmetic. She would make sure that Sally and Susan were not hanging around, giggling, when she was trying to concentrate.

***

The next day, Nancy found herself all of a dither. She had always wanted to teach adults; children were such a nuisance unless under very firm control. Mr. Watson had tutored the sons of gentlefolk in the past, but nobody could remember whether the young men had passed their examinations or not. Nancy was sure that she would be an excellent tutor, but it was difficult to get started in a man's world. Perhaps if Benjie was seen to do very well, she would have other customers.

Nancy had prepared for her first lesson with Benjie, and had thought of nothing else for the past few days. She brought chalk and slates for his arithmetic and a copybook so that he could practice his writing. She had great difficulty in choosing something for him to read, and she brought a selection of books from her classroom. Sally and Susan had been sent out on errands, and she had given them a little money to buy ribbon. Nancy hoped that it would take them a while to choose it.

She tidied up the house, and made sure that she was looking her best – she was just admiring herself in the mirror when Benjie arrived. Her hair was still bright and curly; Nancy would never need curl papers like Jeannie. The freckles had faded once she started spending more time indoors. She studied herself critically, thinking of the corseted ladies Jeannie had told her about. Nancy had always been sturdy; she supposed that a blacksmith's daughter was never going to be pale and slender and she certainly didn't fancy any tight lacings.

"It's very good of you to help me, Miss Graham," said Benjie, making Nancy jump. His deep melodious voice made her go weak at the knees.

"We had better make a start," said Nancy, hoping her voice was not shaking too much. "How much schooling have you had already?"

"I went to Sunday School until my mother died. Once father and I went to live with my grandmother I was not allowed to go to school anymore. I had to start work straight away, even on Sundays. I learnt to read the Bible, and do a bit of arithmetic. I can print, but never learnt to join the letters up properly."

"Try these sums," said Nancy, writing on the slate.

Benjie managed addition fairly easily, without using his fingers to count on.

He progressed quickly to hundreds, tens and units. Subtraction was a little more difficult, until he got the hang of 'borrowing a ten' and 'leaving it on the doorstep', so Nancy gave him one or two more examples to practice on. Benjie could remember his two and three times tables, so Nancy wrote out the four, five and six times tables for practice before the next lesson.

Nancy handed Benjie a book of poetry, for him to choose one to write out and read to her. She observed him while he was writing, his head bent over the slate so that she could not see his wonderful blue eyes or slow distracting smile. It was amazing that he had lived with his grandmother so long without his spirit breaking as Benjie was cheerful, never surly, and always gave her the respect due. Nancy had to pull herself together to look at the writing. They did a little practise with the copybook; she gave him exercises to practise for next time. Nancy thought she was doing very well to keep herself under control and concentrate on the job in hand.

It was much more difficult to keep her mind on the job when Benjie was reading his sonnet out loud; she listened as though in a dream. It felt as if he really meant everything the love poem said; nobody had ever recited love poetry to her before. Here she was, practically an engaged woman; her thoughts were most inappropriate! As soon as he had finished, she handed Benjie a Bible, skipped quickly past unsuitable passages, and asked him to read the twenty-third Psalm.

"I remember this one from Sunday School," said Benjie, and started to read. Nancy was correct in thinking that Benjie was slightly less distracting when he read the Bible, rather than poetry.

"Please keep the Bible," she said, "for reading practice in between lessons." After he had gone, she sang as she gathered up the work. She did not wipe the slate with the poem, but kept it hidden under her pillow. She was still singing when Sally and Susan returned.

Sally and Susan had been to see Mary Ann, and had forgotten one of their errands. They were very surprised that Nancy was in a good mood and did not shout at them; they could not remember her singing in the house before.

"It must be love," said Susan. "Life might be a little more peaceful now Dr. Tom is back from his travels." Sally giggled.

***

Benjie's next lesson followed the same pattern; the arithmetic progressed to pounds, shillings and pence and there was further writing practice. His writing had improved a great deal. Nancy did not go anywhere near the poetry this time, much as she would have liked to. Benjie's voice even made the multiplication tables sound wonderful, and she felt an overwhelming urge to touch him. The sound of her father and his workers in the forge held her back, and she was glad of it; she would not be doing her job properly if she couldn't keep her hands off her pupil. She wondered if she was falling in love, surely not, an educated woman like her. But she read in all her books that anyone could fall in love at any time; very inconvenient. That was for mill girls and dressmakers, not her. Nancy was sure she was made of sterner stuff, just as long as the Bible reading wasn't from the Song of Songs.

After the lesson, she couldn't resist asking Benjie about something that was on her mind.

"I hear that the doctors have a new apprentice."

"That's what I heard."

"Do you know anything about him? Is he local?"

"I don't think so."

"Why the secrecy?"

"I am not sure," said Benjie. "But Tom's sister has a tendency to gossip, and, begging your pardon, your sisters spend a lot of time with her."

Honour was satisfied. Nancy knew that Mary Ann had always been a gossip, always getting Sally and Susan into trouble in class. That must be why Tom hadn't told her; she would have a few words with him on Sunday. Before he went, Benjie gave Nancy a small piece of horse brass; she kept it under her pillow and took it out secretly to polish it.

***

Nancy blinked in the sunshine as she came out of church the following Sunday. All week she felt that she was walking on air, her awareness of her surroundings very much heightened. She had lived in the small Cumberland town all her life, but never noticed the brightness of the flowers, the beauty of the birdsong, the buzzing of the insects, the heady scent of the honeysuckle. Everyone seemed in a particularly good temper, even though the twins looked at her as if they were a bit puzzled. Perhaps it was the sunshine that improved her mood, but yesterday's rain seemed refreshing and did not dampen her spirits.

However, Tom needed to be put in his place.

"I hear you have a new apprentice," said Nancy. "I am disappointed that I had to find out from village gossip."

"I am sorry about that."

"Our local lads were not good enough, and you had to find someone from outside the parish without even telling me."

"It's a bit complicated."

"I don't know how it can be so complicated that you couldn't tell me."

"It is done now," said Tom "If I had known you felt so strongly, I would have said something earlier. I have had a very busy week." He knew better than to say that it was 'man's business. "I am glad you mentioned our apprentice, because I would like to ask your help with young Charlie."

"You want my help now, do you?"

"Charlie could do with a little bit more schooling; could you fit another boy into your top class in the mornings next term? Charlie will be working in the afternoons and the practice will pay for his lessons."

I am not sure about that, thought Nancy, I don't want Tom to think I will just carry out his orders. A strange lad could be disruptive; the top class is bad enough as it is. But the lad that was running up to Tom looked the image of Benjie, only smaller.

"That will be fine, "she said. "We can fit Charlie in."

Tom noticed that Charlie was carrying the doctor's bag.

"Sorry, I have been called out, I won't be able to go for a walk with you this week." But Nancy was not listening.

9 THE FARM

Tom walked towards Charlie, but Nancy had made no move to detain him or ask when she would see him again. Tom would be spared all her questions until his brother's wedding the next Saturday.

"Sorry, Dr. Harrison, they need a doctor at the farm on the hill," said Charlie. "I have brought your bag and everything."

"What is the problem?" asked Tom when they were out of earshot of the crowd.

"One of the haymakers has been taken ill; someone thought that he had fallen off the cart."

"Is everything in the bag you are carrying?"

"Dr. Jarvis packed it for you."

"You had better come with me to watch and learn. It won't take us long to walk to the farm."

They found an old man lying at the edge of the field, out of the sun and away from the continuing work. Tom thought the workers must be from Ma Armstrong's gang; nobody else would be making hay on a Sunday.

"The farmer called you in, not us. We did not send for a doctor. You must send your bill to the farmer, not us," said Fat Frank, the foreman, when he came up. "I want this man patched up so that he can drive his cart. It is all that he is fit for."

The old man opened his eyes, looked around, and lay back with a sigh.

"There is nothing wrong with you," said Frank. I expect you back at work directly."

"What happened?" asked Tom.

"Fell off his cart. Lucky for him that the horse and cart are not damaged," said Frank. He strode off to deal with an imagined slacker at the other side of the field.

"What is your name?" asked Tom.

"Bennett. They called me Wiggy Bennett ever since I went to sea. We had names like Nobby Hall, Chalky White, and Wiggy Bennett. Not always Jack

Tar," said Wiggy.

"You fell off the cart?"

"My leg was hurting and I came over a bit dizzy."

"Let me have a look at your leg," said Tom. Wiggy's right leg was black and swollen, there was a deep cut that had festered and the man looked exhausted.

"That looks a deep cut; how did you hurt your leg?"

"I got in the way of Frank's scythe," said Wiggy. "Can you save my leg, doctor?"

"I am sorry, I can't." said Tom hesitatingly, hating to say it, "I might be able to save your life if I cut your leg off, but it could already be too late. If I spare your leg, it will certainly poison the rest of you."

"Then let me die in one piece," said Wiggy.

"Sailor Jim got around on his wooden leg for quite a few years."

"He had his family to look after him, and didn't have to work. I wouldn't be able to work for Ma; she would send me to the poorhouse. They tell me that life is terrible in there, and I would be ashamed to take charity."

Tom signalled to Charlie and he came over with the doctor's bag.

"A few drops of this will make the pain easier. My lad here will stay with you while I talk to the farmer. Wiggy, please don't tell my lad too many exciting tales of life at sea, I don't want him running off."

Wiggy looked at Charlie and his face lit up. "Benjie!" he said.

"I never thought to see you! Don't work for Ma, go to sea, anything! I know she is your grandmother but she works her gang too hard. She gets most of the men from the poorhouse, and works them until they are old and no use to her anymore. She keeps all the money, and doesn't feed her workers right," said Wiggy. "Don't stay with Ma, you will either die young like your father or end up like me."

Wiggy closed his eyes and never spoke again. Charlie didn't get a chance to say that he wasn't Benjie.

***

Tom and Charlie were silent as they walked back to the surgery, then Tom set Charlie to continue tidying the back room while he talked to William.

"Did you save your patient?" asked William.

"No, it was too late, the wound had festered too much. Sometimes all you can do is make the patient comfortable," said Tom.

"Wasn't the wound recent?"

"It looked about a fortnight old, and had been neglected. The man was ready to go."

"Could he have been saved if we had treated him earlier?"

"If we had seen him right away, and he had been allowed to rest his leg, or if Frank had been more careful with his scythe in the first place."

"What were the factors contributing to the death?"

"The blow with the scythe gave him the wound, the neglect allowed infection to set in and the overwork did not help. He died of gangrene rather than the fall from the cart."

"Are there any witnesses to say that it was Frank's scythe?"

"No, we have only Wiggy's word for it. Apparently he told the farmer how it happened. Hearsay is not evidence, and no-one is going to say, under oath, that Wiggy was physically prevented from medical assistance. But my report must reflect what I saw, if it is to be an honest one. What do you think the Coroner's verdict will be?"

"Misadventure, or it could even be Natural Causes or Old Age. It ought to be manslaughter, but there is not enough evidence. All we can hope for is that the Coroner recommends more care of the gang members. The advice would probably be ignored, but the Coroner might remember if there had been doubt in a similar case. I suppose Wiggy is to have a pauper's funeral; he has no relatives, and Ma doesn't pay for her workers' funerals. There are too many."

"The government is thinking of bringing in a law to say that paupers' corpses can be anatomized," continued William. "Apparently there aren't enough murderers, and everyone is watching the churchyards, and medical schools need the bodies. So a man works hard all his life, goes to church, says his prayers, but he can't go to heaven because his body is all in separate bits somewhere."

"Don't dwell on it, it probably won't happen," said Tom. "If it comes to it, I won't cut anyone up unless I am absolutely sure they are going to hell anyway."

"How can you tell? They may have made a deathbed repentance."

"Perhaps my anatomizing days are over, I certainly learnt a lot in Edinburgh. I wish I had been called in early enough to save Wiggy. He was a nice old boy."

"We've all that learning and we can't save our patients."

"We help most of them," said Tom. "And we can't save the whole town. Some of the patients have such awful lives that they meet death halfway. I shall make a full report to the Coroner and he may make recommendations."

"Too little, too slow," said William, the reformer.

"You helped my sister Elizabeth," said Tom, the pragmatist. "My parents wouldn't have listened to me. Elizabeth is going to stay with our brother Joe in Hilltop after George's wedding.

" What would we be if we couldn't help our own?" said William, sinking into his usual gloom; he had a very bleak view of the world sometimes. Tom could see that this could be another evening where William would drink too much brandy and get a bit maudlin in his cups. But he seemed a little brighter since Charlie's arrival.

It was quite late when Tom finished his report, so he decided to see Benjie the next day. Bad news could always wait.

The next morning, Tom decided to check up on Charlie's activities and he was not pleased to see two extra jars on the shelves in the back room, next to the specimens.

"What's in this jar, Charlie?"

"Caterpillars. I didn't know I wasn't allowed pets. I will look after them and feed them and everything. I like it when they turn into butterflies and fly away. I didn't think an extra jar would make a difference in here."

Tom sighed. "And what do caterpillars eat?"

"Leaves, sir. I pick them from your little garden out the back."

"And which leaves do they like best?"

"They like these cabbages best. It's funny, that!"

"And who are the cabbages supposed to be for?"

"For us. Very sorry Dr. Tom."

"Dr. Jarvis particularly likes cabbages," said Tom. "He spent a lot of time building up a vegetable garden when he was a well man."

"Very sorry, I'll set the caterpillars free right away, and I will look after the garden for Dr. Jarvis. I'm really grateful to you both for giving me a chance. I could have ended up like Wiggy Bennett," said Charlie, picking up the jar.

"Right away from our garden, if you please."

Charlie ran off, and quickly returned. Tom didn't ask whose garden had gained some caterpillars.

"And what is in this other jar?"

"Tadpoles, sir. Shall I set them free as well?"

"No, frogs will be useful, they will eat slugs and snails from the garden. This is not a good place to keep tadpoles, they would be better in the bruce when you have cleaned it out."

"What's the bruce?" asked Charlie.

"The little outbuilding between the privy and the washhouse. Many houses were built with a brew house for making beer and wine, but they don't use them much now."

"You make beer from malt and hops, but what do you make wine from?"

"Surplus vegetables or fruit. There is a book on it somewhere here," said Tom, waving his hands vaguely towards the shelves.

"Damsons?" asked Charlie.

"They make good wine," said Tom, hiding a smile. Wine would not help William's problem any, but he did not think Charlie would get very far. In the meantime, it would give Charlie some practice with his reading and arithmetic.

"I would like you to stay in the shop until Dr. Jarvis gets up. Write down what the customers ask for. Dr Jarvis or I will make up the medicine and you can deliver it. And no picking your nose when you are sitting in the shop, it puts the customers off. I have a couple of visits to make," he said, as he walked towards the door.

***

"Have you come for your horse, Dr. Tom?" asked Benjie. "He is stabled her , so you can call for him whenever you like. I have the extra saddlebags you asked for."

" Not today, but it'll be very useful now I am making more visits," said Tom. "I'll save a lot of time." He looked up at Thunderbolt, and wished he had chosen Dobbin instead.

"Perhaps you would like to put him through his paces now, while it is quiet. Just to get used to him, like."

Tom gulped, but he mounted fairly easily. Thunderbolt didn't seem quite so big from this angle.

"I came to tell you some sad news about Wiggy Bennett," said Tom as they walked their horses sedately along a quiet farm track

"I heard that he died at Hill Farm yesterday," said Benjie. "We will miss him; he was very good to me when my father died."

"Wiggy asked for you but we hadn't time to fetch you. He spoke to your cousin instead; there is such a strong family resemblance between you and Charlie that he thought he was speaking to you. Wiggy gave our apprentice a lot of advice and told him why he should never work for Ma's gang."

"Too late for me. I expect they will want me to look after the horse and cart now Wiggy has gone. But I am really grateful that you took Charlie on. How is he doing?"

"He is a hard worker, very eager to please; he is learning quickly. He is much more suitable than the lads at the school, and we can trust him to look after the shop for Dr. Jarvis when I am out on my rounds," said Tom, as they broke into a trot. He did not say that Charlie needed more schooling or that it was sometimes hard work keeping up with his high spirits and energy. Tom supposed he must have been like that himself, but it was a long time ago and he couldn't remember.

"How about a canter across this field?" asked Benjie.

Tom felt good, and even better when the canter turned into a gallop. He felt free at last, from his worries about William and the practice. He felt free from the gossip and chatter of the womenfolk, always asking him questions about what he was doing and where he was going. He knew he should be living at home, but found William and Charlie's company much more restful. Tom certainly wasn't ready for a household of his own, especially with a wife like Nancy. As a bachelor, he could go where he liked, when he liked, and not have to answer questions all the time. Out here there was only Benjie's quiet company, and Thunderbolt was his ride to freedom.

10 THE FARMHAND

One of the men at Wiggy's funeral had told Benjie that the gang was finding it difficult to cope with the horse and cart. The horse was pining for Wiggy, and frightened of Frank – the goods on the cart had a very bumpy ride. Ma felt sure that they were losing money when they had to stop to collect things that had fallen off.

Ma and Frank caught up with Benjie when he was going back to the stables from the forge, but he already knew what was coming.

"We need you back on the gang tomorrow morning."

"Mr. Brown wants me to stay and work for him."

"He might do, but I am your legal guardian until you are twenty-one and I say where you will work. I am very surprised that you don't want to work for your old gran," said Ma. Frank didn't say anything, he just loomed.

"My boss needs me here, to look after the stables," said Benjie "You can talk to him when he gets back." He knew they had seen Mr. Brown leave for Carlisle and picked their time to pay Benjie a visit. "He told me to look after the horses until he got back."

"Don't you dare argue with me! If you are not ready to start work first thing tomorrow morning, I will send Frank and some of the others to get you."

Benjie swallowed and nodded.

"And you can forget about all that book learning. You won't need it now. I know that you have been getting your feet under the table at the blacksmith's. Their fancy ways are not for the likes of you."

As soon as they had gone, Benjie started walking up to the blacksmith's, carrying his slates and copybook. After a great deal of thought, he brought his Bible with him. He wanted to keep it; he had never had a book of his own before. He had started to read from the beginning and had got as far as the exciting bit with Joshua and all the battles; he would love to know what happened next.

Benjie knew that he would have no safe place to keep any possessions once he got back home and he didn't want to risk his one book being destroyed. He was always sorry to go back home after the freedom of being hired out, and this time he had enjoyed it so much more. Benjie always loved working in the stables, getting to know the different horses and looking after them. He was always in trouble at home for giving extra hay to their horse, and for making his life as easy as possible. Star worked much better for Benjie; surprisingly this did not seem to please Frank either.

There was no way of Benjie getting away for lessons at Nancy's as he would have no regular free time, probably no free time at all. Benjie realized that he would miss his lessons; he enjoyed the reading and the satisfaction of getting his sums right. The writing practice was a bit boring, but he could see the improvement in his copybook. His boss would have given him a job on the strength of it, but Ma wanted him back in the gang and there was nothing either of them could do.

Nancy was so different from the kind of women Benjie was used to. Nancy was beautiful, kind and gentle. She was dainty in her ways, and with her high-class language she sounded like a real lady. Benjie was amazed that someone so far above him should take an interest in him and help him so much. He had offered pennies for the schooling, out of his tips at the inn. Nancy had refused, saying that it was a pleasure to teach him. Benjie had heard Nancy's name linked with Dr. Tom, the surgeon, and thought she would make him a lovely wife. Not for the likes of Benjie, though, Ma was right about that.

Benjie was so busy thinking about Nancy that he didn't realize that he was almost at the forge. The blacksmith, Richard, had just arrived back home. Benjie helped him settle his horse, and they went into the house together.

***

"Why are you so late?" Nancy asked her father. She saw Benjie with him and added, "…we were worried about you, father. Did you have a good journey?"

"The journey was fine. The blacksmith at Gretna was busy when we got there, so the start of the game was delayed," said Richard. "Pour the tea, please, Nancy, it has been a long day. Will you stay for tea, Benjie?"

"I'm not sure," said Benjie. He had never been invited to tea before, and didn't know if his manners were up to it. He knew tea was hot and had to be sipped slowly. The bread and cakes looked wonderful, but all that china made him nervous.

"Please stay for tea, Benjie," said Nancy, smiling at him. Susan giggled and looked at Sally.

"I can stay for a little while, said Benjie "but I won't be able to come for any more lessons. They need me to work in the gang from tomorrow. I have to go back home tonight."

"Will you be able to come back after the harvest?" asked Nancy.

"I don't know where they will send me this winter. Usually we are digging ditches and laying hedges after the potato picking is over. I have brought my books back, I have nowhere to keep them at home," said Benjie. He was surprised to see Nancy looking upset; she must like her teaching very much. Sally and Susan looked at each other.

There was a knock on the door; when Susan opened it Charlie was standing in the doorway, clutching a large bottle.

"I've brought your jollop from the doctor, Mr. Graham," said Charlie.

"Come in and sit down, Charlie," said Richard. Sally made room for him on the bench, and Nancy poured out another cup of tea. Charlie slurped his tea noisily but Benjie hadn't touched his. He was so pleased to see that his cousin was working for the doctors; it was all he could have hoped for.

"Are you two related?" asked Sally, looking from Charlie to Benjie and back again. "You look very alike."

"What a question to ask, Sally!" said Richard.

"Charlie is my first cousin on my father's side," said Benjie as he found his voice." I'm so pleased to see you looking so well, Charlie. His face broke into a broad grin as they shook hands. "Life at the apothecary shop must suit you."

"Yes, I realize how lucky I am. Dr. Jarvis and Dr. Tom went to the poorhouse to see if there were any boys that could start work straight away, and they chose me," said Charlie.

"I never thought of going to the poorhouse for an apprentice," said Richard. "I might just try it; the boys from the school are too frightened of Miss Nancy here and might not like to work for me."

"How could that possibly be?" asked Benjie. "Miss Graham is a wonderfully kind teacher." Sally and Susan were giggling. "The children must love her; how could they ever be afraid?" Sally managed to hide her face in her handkerchief but Susan had to leave the table for a few minutes.

"Are there any more lads in the poorhouse?" asked Richard.

"Kit Dawson is my age, but really big and strong; he sometimes works with the men." said Charlie.

"What can Kit do?" asked Richard.

Charlie thought about Kit trying to write his name, holding a pencil in his thick fingers. Kit's day in the tailor's shop was even less successful. Charlie frantically tried to think of something that Kit was good at.

"Kit is better at throwing stones than anyone I know," said Charlie.

"I don't see how that would be any help," said Nancy, but Richard looked thoughtful.

"Did our men win the game of quoits?" asked Susan.

"No, we didn't, we just haven't got enough younger men coming on board," said Richard. "It is a real local derby, and our men have always won in the past. Our tactics made up for the fact that we are getting a bit old; we were known for it, until today. Their team captain was busy, so we couldn't start right away."

"What was he doing?" asked Susan.

"The Gretna blacksmith holds weddings at his forge," said Richard. "So when a young couple arrived, Hamish had to find the anvil priest and help with the wedding. It took a bit longer this time because the bride's father turned up before the anvil priest. So they had to make it look as if he was too late to stop the wedding."

"How did they do that?" asked Susan.

"Never you mind," said Richard. Benjie and Charlie looked at each other and tried to keep their faces straight.

"Why do they hold weddings at the forge?" asked Sally.

"In England the bride and groom have to be over twenty-one to marry without parent's consent. In Scotland bride and groom can marry without parent's consent as long as they are both over sixteen. English couples that didn't want to wait to get married started going to Gretna, as it is just over the border. Their inns and shops do quite well out of the extra trade, so they can't turn it down. In fact, they encourage it," said Richard.

"Don't they have to read the banns for four weeks before a wedding?" asked Nancy, thinking of her friend Jeannie's wedding the following day.

"They don't have to live in the parish or anything, they can get married as soon as the anvil priest turns up. So if Susan or Sally decided to run off with young Charlie here at the age of sixteen, I wouldn't be able to stop them," said Richard.

"How exciting," said Susan, "Shame you lost your game, though."

"Yes we will have to start practising for the return match at harvest time," said Richard. "Charlie, did you say your friend Kit was good at throwing stones?"

"He never misses," said Charlie.

After tea the conversation kept coming back to the game of quoits.

"I don't see why grown men spend their time throwing horseshoes on to a peg at the other side of the green," said Nancy.

"We use proper quoits in a real game, we only use horseshoes when we are practising," said Richard, who had had this conversation many times before. "And the peg is called a hob."

"And why can't they just stand nearer to the peg to make it easier?"

"Those are the rules of the game. I have explained all this before."

"Then why are the rules different when you go to different inns?"

"Women find it difficult to follow the differences between the Scottish and the Northern game," said Benjie. "Begging your pardon, Miss Graham." Richard gasped; nobody had ever said that to her before. "Would you like me to explain it to you?"

"Please do, I have always wanted to know."

At this point Sally and Susan said they had just remembered they had promised to go and see Mary Ann, and would it be all right if they did the washing up later. Richard was very amused by the turn of the conversation and Charlie was working his way through a large pile of toast.

"The game they play in Scotland is called 'The Long Game' and the players have to throw eighteen yards instead of eleven. And the quoits are much bigger, nine inches instead of five and a half. Heavier too, eleven pounds instead of five pounds."

"And are all the quoits exactly the same everywhere in England?" She loved to hear Benjie's voice, even when he recited the multiplication tables.

"The quoits can vary in weight a bit between the different inns. At the Queen's Arms the quoits weigh five and a half pounds; Arthur Brown looks after them. His father says they are the correct weight and all the other inns have got it wrong."

"That is not so much of a difference, I don't see what all the fuss is about."

"In Scotland, the hob is called the pin, and it is flush with the ground. It makes the game a lot simpler, as there is no advantage in encircling the pin. And each quoit matters, not just the top one. Just brute force and ignorance really, not like our clever game."

"Do you play?"

"I play as 'shower up' sometimes when they are short of players."

"That's the player that stands by the hob and shouts encouragement to the thrower," said Charlie, through a mouthful of toast. "I would love to do that."

"A lot of men standing around and arguing, and then they go in for their ale," said Nancy "All men's games are like that."

"I suppose I have to go soon, the doctors are expecting me back now I have finished my errands," said Charlie.

"I heard that Wiggy spoke to you before he died," said Benjie.

"Yes, he must have thought he was talking to you. He said not to work in the gang because Ma works her gang too hard, until they are too old and no use to her anymore. She keeps most of the money and doesn't feed her workers right. He said you would die young like your father or end up like Wiggy himself," said Charlie, looking at the stricken faces." Sorry, but that is what he said."

"It is all right, I am used to the farm work, and I like looking after the horse. I might get a few minutes free; can I call and see you at the shop.”

“Yes, sometimes I am stuck in that shop all day when Dr. Jarvis is busy and Dr. Tom is on his rounds.”

“Only in the afternoons after harvest,” said Nancy, “You will be in my school in the mornings.”

“Yes, Miss,” said Charlie giving her his best smile before he ran off home.

“He is lucky to get the chance, I will miss my lessons,” said Benjie as he stood at the door with Nancy and Richard.

“Perhaps you might have half an hour to spare sometimes in the evening,” said Nancy. “It would be a shame if you forgot everything you learnt and we had to start all over again next year.”

“I could do with more sums, multiplying, weights and measures, things like that,” said Benjie. “And more handwriting practice, I suppose.”

“Could you get away at all?”

“We all go into the ale house when we get paid; no one would miss me for half an hour or so, I can’t promise exactly when, though.”

“I’ll keep your books ready for you here,” said Nancy “For whenever you manage to come.”

“Why did you have to go back to the gang; didn’t your boss want you to stay there?” asked Richard.

“Yes, but Ma Armstrong is my legal guardian and I must work for her until I am of age. The time will go quickly,” said Benjie.

“Seems a pity, especially after what Wiggy advised. Unless some young lady runs off to Gretna Green with you!” said Richard.

“I am hoping for offers,” said Benjie, trying to keep the mood light as he went reluctantly back. The last hour at the blacksmith’s seemed a world away from his future life as one of the gang of farm labourers. Nancy managed to hide her blushes from Benjie and from her father.

11 THE HEN NIGHT

Nancy felt there would be a big gap in her life without Benjie's lessons twice a week, as she had spent a lot of her time thinking and planning for them. Grown-ups were easier to teach than children; it must be good to teach people who really wanted to learn. Nancy had hoped that when people saw Benjie's progress, students would all want to learn from her. But now it looked as if there would never be enough adult lessons to make a living, which was a pity, because children were such a nuisance.

Sally and Susan ran up, all out of breath. Nancy knew that they must have been telling Mary Ann all about Gretna Green weddings. Then Mary Ann would tell the rest of the class, embellishing the facts as she went along.

"Mary Ann and Elizabeth have been to see Jeannie about their dresses for the wedding," said Sally.

"Mary Ann has to have her dress let down," said Susan. "She is going to be tall like her brother Tom."

"Elizabeth has to have her dress taken in a bit," said Sally.

"Perhaps you ought to try your dress on when you collect it," said Susan "in case it doesn't fit."

"I've already collected my dress. Of course it fits, why wouldn't it?" said Nancy, trying to box Susan's ears. Susan dodged and both twins giggled.

***

Nancy walked towards Jeannie's house, as it suddenly occurred to her that Jeannie might need a bit of help. The night before a wedding should be spent in beauty sleep, not making last minute alterations to other people's dresses. Nancy felt that her fellow bridesmaids had been very inconsiderate.

49

Jeannie was shorter than Nancy, with brown eyes and straight dark hair. She looked a little flustered.

"I heard that you were busy and came to see if you needed any help with the sewing," said Nancy.

"I would appreciate that," said Jeannie. "Can you do Mary Ann's hem for me? It is pinned to the right length. Then I can concentrate on the difficult bits on Elizabeth's dress."

"Shall I get the flat irons ready for pressing?" asked Nancy. She was more used to taking charge than taking orders.

"The irons are already heating up. It would be wonderful if you could just do Mary Ann's hem, then I will have time to curl my hair for tomorrow."

"Is this the one?" asked Nancy, picking up a dress. She noticed that Jeannie was doing the more interesting part of the work, and delegating the boring bit. Even some of the girls in her class had progressed beyond hemming. She supposed that Jeannie was a qualified dressmaker and knew what she was doing but Nancy had always preferred to be in control, and never liked taking orders. Still, as chief bridesmaid she had responsibilities to make sure that the bride was not going to be too tired on her wedding day.

"Thank you," said Jeannie. "The needles and thread are in this work box here. I will be glad when they invent machines to do some of the stitching."

"Machines like in the mill?" asked Nancy," wouldn't they be too big?"

"I heard that someone had invented a small machine with a treadle for the dressmaker to work it. No coal, no steam, no noise, no mess."

"What happened?"

"It didn't work properly and they spent more time untangling the thread than they would have spent sewing in the first place. But it is only a matter of time before they get it right."

"Are you going to do dressmaking after you are married?"

"Yes, but I'll do it at home. I have my own private customers now, and there is always plenty of work. The gentlemen's wives always want extra dresses and alterations so that everything is in the latest fashion."

"Are their dresses like ours, but with better quality material?"

"Partly. But their dresses have more corseting, as they are a more difficult shape," said Jeannie, pointing to a half finished dress on a stand.

"They can't really be that shape!"

"Not to start with. They have to pull the laces really tight, it must be very uncomfortable."

"I think I can remember Tom saying something about that when he came back from Carlisle. I don't see how the ladies can breathe, or how they can get any work done."

"They don't need to work; they just have to look decorative. And lie on a chaise longue. They faint sometimes."

"I couldn't be doing with that. If I had my way they would stop being silly and do a decent day's work."

"We dressmakers need to keep the ladies idle, so that we get their custom."

"I notice that the mill is not quite as busy as it was. They only took on four lads from our top class."

"George hardly ever gets overtime now. There will always be work for blacksmiths like your dad, but millwork can vary. That is the main reason why I will carry on working. There is always a demand for dresses to be made or changed; women always want to change how they look. And printed calico is very cheap, thanks to the mill."

"I hadn't thought whether I would work after I get married. I suppose the school board wouldn't allow it, which is a pity."

"You wouldn't need to earn money; Tom will always be in work, and you would just look after the house. I suppose you would have to fit in with Tom; is he still living at the shop?"

"Just for the time being, he says, until the apprentice has settled in. Dr. Jarvis has been poorly, but he seems to be getting better. I think if Tom organized things a bit better, he could live at home with his mother and father." Nancy thought of how she would change things at the shop, to make life more convenient for herself.

"Tom seems quite comfortable there, it is a real bachelor establishment. George and I have a lovely little house, near my mother. One big room downstairs, and a bedroom upstairs. The neighbours are nice."

"Is everything ready for the wedding tomorrow?" asked Nancy, before Jeannie went into detail on the house.

"Yes, except that we are not quite sure where the dancing is going to be. We would like it to be on the green at the back of the Queen's Arms, but Arthur wants to get the green ready for the next match. I am really looking forward to being with George all the time instead of just Sundays."

"When you promise to obey him tomorrow, does that mean you will always have to do as he says?"

"Mostly," said Jeannie. "Men have more experience of the world than we have. All we know is this small town, our work and our families. Your Tom has even lived in Edinburgh so he knows everything that goes on in big cities."

"Knowledge does not always mean common sense," said Nancy. She was not sure that she would want to obey Tom. She felt that he should listen to her sometimes, for his own good.

"At the moment George and I are living in our parents' houses, but things will be different when we have our own little place."

Nancy had been running her father's household for him since she was twelve, and couldn't imagine anyone doing things any other way. Her way was the only sensible way to run a house, and she did not want to compromise. Nancy thought that Tom lived in a very haphazard manner in the shop. Tom needed regular hours, a bit of organization, and less time spent at the ale house.

"And the rest of the marriage vows?" asked Nancy.

"I want to love and cherish George all my life," said Jeannie." how is that hem going?"

"Nearly finished," said Nancy, speeding up," I will help you curl your hair if you like." She couldn't imagine herself caring for Tom in the same way that Jeannie was going to look after George. For some reason she suddenly thought of Benjie – now he could use some cherishing.

"Then I can get my beauty sleep," said Jeannie. "I wonder what George is doing now."

12 THE STAG NIGHT

George was in the Queen's Arms with brothers Joe, Tom and Robert. The landlord's son, Arthur, was worrying about the green behind the ale house.

"If there's dancing on the green tomorrow, it won't be in a fit state for the big quoits match," said Arthur.

"The match is ages yet," said George.

"Only a few weeks," said Arthur. "I work hard on that green for the quoits match, not for you to dance on. The grass got all churned up last time."

"There'll be plenty of time for the grass to grow again, if it needs to. We get enough rain," said Tom.

"The green has to be right for the match. Then they can't say we are cheating with extra humps and hollows. It might not rain," said Arthur.

"There'll be plenty of rain between now and harvest time, there always is. Anyway we haven't even got a full team," said Tom.

"I heard that the blacksmith is training up his new apprentice, a very promising player. Surprised Nancy hadn't told you," said Arthur.

"Things haven't changed at all here, Arthur is still like an old woman about his quoits green," said Robert "It is good to be back."

"The green has to be right, the honour of the town is at stake," said Arthur.

"Of course it has, and I'm sure it will be fine on the day," said Tom, frowning at his young brother, Robert. "I hear you went off to Durham to be a miner".

"I changed my mind because there is so much other work in the area. There is an exciting new invention near Darlington, called the railway. They have built an engine that can pull much more weight than a horse can. The engine can't run on the roads; it has to have its own special railway tracks. I am working as a platelayer, laying and mending the tracks," said Robert.

"What does the engine run on?" asked Tom.

"They burn coal to make steam, the steam drives the engine pulling the wagons, neat as you please. It is much quicker to build a railway than a canal, and the loads can be moved more quickly," said Robert.

"It's all very well for Darlington," said Tom "I am not sure that we would want a railway here."

"Could the railway bring lots of coal from Newcastle to the mill?" asked George.

"They could build a railway anywhere. Only problem is they have to ask parliament every time they want to extend the track. It can take a while for people to make fine speeches and decide things," said Robert.

"I can't see them running a railway in Westmorland. Our weather would put the fire out straight away. Even if they could build a track to go up our fells, the engine would be stranded if there were a landslide or big snowdrift. Horses will always find a way around," said Joe.

"The engine will have to stop when it runs out of coal, but a horse will work when it is hungry," said Tom. "And know its way home."

"We will get no peace until we go outside and admire Tom's horse," said Robert.

"I thought you would never ask," said Tom.

***

Thunderbolt was admired, and put through his paces, although George and Arthur had seen it all before. Back inside, with another jug of ale, Joe and Robert were suitably impressed.

"He looks sound, but I have seen faster horses," said Joe.

"Travelling a short distance by horse is unnecessary," said Robert. "Unless you need Thunderbolt to take you home when you are in no fit state to walk."

"I can hold my ale as well as you can," said Tom.

"There must be profit in ale," said George.

"Not much," said Arthur. "We have a lot of responsibilities, what with all the coach travel. We have to look after the travellers, rooms for the night, extra food and the like. And there are fights in the ale house to sort out."

"That's usually my job," said Tom. "I am often here to patch men up on market days."

"There are a lot that we manage to stop before they get that far," said Arthur.

"Very commendable," said Joe.

"Trying to avoid damage to the inn," said Arthur.

"I work at one of the ale houses at Hilltop," said Joe. "There is a long winter with no farm labouring work."

"How is Alice?" asked Tom.

"She is well, but gets lonely when I am working in the evenings," said Joe "She'll be really glad that Elizabeth is travelling back with us, she will be glad of her company."

"So you are to be a married man, George," said Arthur. "I wonder which of your brothers will be next?"

"It should have been Tom before me," said George "as he is older. But every time I mention Nancy, he goes all quiet."

Tom explained why he thought that he was not in a position to marry.

"I think you are enjoying bachelor life too much "said George. "But who does the housekeeping at your shop?"

"We've someone to do the shopping and cleaning and she takes our washing on Mondays. Charlie cooks a bit, or fetches pies for us. So there is no one to complain if we get blood on our shirts or want meals at odd times," said Tom.

"Nancy wouldn't stand for that," said Robert, laughing. Tom's face clouded over. He had been thinking the same thing.

"Nancy is a lovely girl," said Tom. "One day we will settle down."

"She won't wait for ever," said Joe.

"Nancy doesn't seem to be in a hurry," said Tom. "But mother is pushing. She wants us all married and settled down."

"Nancy has been giving Benjie Armstrong some private tutoring. I heard it first from Mary Ann, but Jeannie says the same," said George.

"Has she now!" said Tom as his face brightened.

"It looks as if I might be the next brother to be married," said Robert.

"I didn't know you were courting," said George.

"I wasn't, not really, "said Robert.

"Why get married then?" asked Tom.

"It looks as if I have no choice. The girls are very forward in Darlington, determined to have their wicked way with me. What's a man to do?" said Robert, posing as a young innocent victim.

"I'll always be the best man, never the groom," said Tom, happily. "Thank you for making all this effort to keep mother happy."

"You're welcome," said Robert. "I think we need another jug of ale."

***

William was still up when Tom walked unsteadily into the shop.

"It looks as if you had a good time," said William.

"There'll be some sore heads in the morning; young Robert was well away," said Tom. "I will have to get up early to make sure that George gets to the church."

"I thought you would stay with your family tonight."

"They have a house full already, so for once there were no complaints about me living at the shop. It's nice and quiet here, and there is more space. And someone might ask for medicine or laudanum. I would hate to lose a sale."

"Charlie and I can manage fine, unless you are looking for an excuse to stay here. What will you do when you are married?"

"The practice needs me here until you are feeling better and Charlie has learnt a bit more."

"Don't make excuses, I could send Charlie to fetch you when you were needed. I managed when you were in Edinburgh."

"Other surgeons sent you their journeymen when I was away."

"Some were more use than others. I know you have more responsibilities now that you are a partner but they should not get in the way of marrying Nancy. What is the real reason? It won't go any further, doctors can keep secrets."

"I love Nancy, of course, but I don't want to live with her just yet. I wouldn't be able to call my soul my own. I might not be able to keep her out of the shop! That back room would be cleaned, swept and tidied until it looked like anywhere else. Us doctors like to keep our mystery."

"Nancy would make you a good wife. She would look after your interests very well."

"For my own good, of course. That's what worries me. I would be more comfortable with a little neglect."

"You don't want to marry her at all, do you?"

"Not really, to be honest. I love her and everything, I suppose."

"Then you must tell her the position, Tom. Leave her free to marry someone else, if you don't want to marry her."

"I will talk to her tomorrow," said Tom, and was surprised to feel relieved.

"If you don't marry, you will become a lonely bitter old man like me. Had you thought of that?"

"I hope to be like you. Why did you never get married?"

"Women are difficult to live with, and childbirth is a worry. I just never got around to courting, and nobody would have me now. Though a rich widow with her own inn would be nice."

"They are like gold dust," said Tom. "If everyone waited for one of those, the human race would die out."

13 THE BRIDESMAID

The wedding was going to be a shambles. Nancy arrived at Jeannie's house, ready for a sedate procession to the church with Jeannie, her father and the bridesmaids making a dignified entrance, before the congregation wondered if anyone had changed their mind. But Jeannie was still fussing over her dress.

Mary Ann and Elizabeth came running up, all out of breath. While Jeannie tidied them up (Mary Ann's hem had come down in a couple of places), she asked them what was wrong.

"George and Robert are sort of poorly, and will be a little bit late," said Elizabeth. "It would be best not to arrive at the church too early, so can we wait a while or walk very slowly."

"It wouldn't do to arrive before the groom, I don't want to appear to be too eager," said Jeannie. "What is the matter with George and Robert?"

"Robert's head hurts and he has been very sick. George is not as bad if he moves slowly and doesn't eat anything." said Mary Ann.

"Has Tom arrived? Is he all right?" asked Nancy.

"Tom is a bit quiet but he is sorting them out, and he gave Robert some medicine. Robert was sick again but felt better afterwards; it's just taking them a while to get ready. All my brothers were at the Queen's Arms last night and they came in very late. Father has gone to the church already for some peace and quiet. Joe and Alice are staying in George's new house so they are missing it all. Mother is shouting at everyone, especially Tom; she blames him for leading Robert astray," said Mary Ann.

"I don't think Jeannie needed to know all that," said Nancy, who saw Robert as more of a ringleader than an innocent victim.

"I think ten or fifteen minute's wait should be enough," said Elizabeth.

Jeannie and her family were very amused by Mary Ann's version of events.

Nancy thought that it was typical Harrison behaviour, and she preferred to distance herself from it.

***

Nancy knew that she looked her best at the wedding; her father had told her. She was so pleased that she pretended not to hear Susan saying that she looked less of a harridan than usual. Jeannie looked radiant, but she kept breaking out into a muffled giggle behind her veil as she thought about the chaos at the Harrisons'. As Jeannie's friend, Nancy was chief bridesmaid, so Mary Ann and Elizabeth had to walk behind her. Children should walk behind their teacher and know their place. Nancy thought she heard whispering somewhere, but wasn't sure.

She loved the wedding, the dressing up, being an important part of the ceremony and the admiration of the crowd. It must be wonderful for Jeannie, to be the centre of attention with everyone making a fuss of her. But her life would be more difficult afterwards; losing her independence and becoming part of the Harrison family. For the first time, Nancy admitted to herself that she did not want the same kind of life as Jeannie. But she did not want to become an old maid, still teaching the same class in forty years' time.

As Nancy stood blinking in the strong sunshine outside the church, she noticed something flying past her and she automatically put up her hand to catch it.

"You caught the bouquet Miss, you will get married next!" shouted Mary Ann. A chorus of children started chanting, "Miss is getting married." Nancy managed to get home before she burst into tears.

***

Nancy thought she would put the flowers in water, make herself a cup of tea and go back when she felt better. But her second cup was empty and she still didn't feel like moving. Nancy was lost in her thoughts and was startled when her father came in.

"I just came back to see how my new apprentice was doing," said Richard.

"He's just playing," said Nancy, looking out of the window at Kit Dawson who was patiently throwing horseshoes on to a peg in the yard. "Didn't you give him any work to do?"

"I asked him to practice his throwing. "He will save the honour of the town one day."

Nancy did not see what that stolid child could contribute; he was sturdy and pleasant enough, but a little slow. For once she did not speak her mind.

"And what are you doing, away from the party?"

"It just didn't feel right."

"Jeannie's wedding or yours?"

"I don't want to marry Tom," said Nancy, as the tears started again." But I don't want to be laughed at for an old maid either."

"Then you must tell Tom and set him free," said Richard, although he had been looking forward to the day when Nancy married. It wasn't just that life would be easier when she left home; he just wanted to see his daughters settled.

"It's difficult; he hasn't actually asked me to marry him."

"Not ever?"

"Only when we were children. If I say anything he'll think I was trying to hold him to it."

"Perhaps you should ask him to NOT marry you," said Richard. "Make a proposal of unmarriage."

Nancy smiled for the first time that day.

"I will stay at home and look after you and my sisters."

Richard wondered how she would feel when Sally and Susan married, but decided not to say anything.

"Is Benjie calling to see us this week?" he asked.

"He will call if he can, but they keep him very busy, I try not to worry but I hope he is alright."

Richard saw a little glimmer of hope. Nancy might be hard to place, but he could always provide a dowry.

***

When Nancy got back to the wedding party, there was chaos. Nobody had put the food out on the plates, but the guests hadn't waited and just started drinking.

"Where's the bride's father?" asked Nancy.

"He had to be helped home," said Mary Ann. "This always happens at weddings. Father said 'this is as it should be.'"

"Not always so early! And the bride's mother?"

"She went to sort him out, make him lie down for a bit. Father is smoking his pipe somewhere, and everyone is avoiding mother."

"Then it's down to us," said Nancy. "We must sort the food out before anyone else goes home."

Sally, Susan and Mary Ann were soon setting the tables, while Nancy went to find the fiddler. She eventually found him asleep in one of the outhouses, jug of ale in one hand and violin in the other. Nancy woke him up, confiscated the ale and told him that he wouldn't get his money unless he made an effort.

When Nancy got back to the party with the fiddler, it just looked like a normal wedding breakfast. The bride's father had made it back, but had to be propped up on both sides as he beamed at everyone at his table.

"People were just standing about, and not getting on with things. They need a leader and I am just the person to do it," said Nancy.

"Everyone seems to think it's the best wedding party ever," said Richard.

"If I make sure that no one starts a food fight, can you make sure that the fiddler doesn't wander off again? I need someone reliable," said Nancy.

***

Later on in the evening, everyone was enjoying the dancing. Nancy searched for Tom, but he was more difficult to find than the fiddler had been. She wondered if he had been avoiding her. She went to the kitchen to refill a cream jug; it was much quicker to do things herself. Sure enough, there was Tom; he had just finished patching two men up after a minor scuffle.

"Where are you going to, my pretty maid?" he asked, as the childhood nursery rhyme sprang to mind. They had sung the rhyme together many years ago.

"I'm going a milking, sir," she said, waving her cream jug.

"What is your fortune, my pretty maid?"

Tom wasn't quite sure where this was leading, but the words came to his mouth automatically.

"My face is my fortune, sir," she said. "And my housekeeping skills, superior teaching ability, wide knowledge and ability to get things done properly".

"Then I can't marry you, my pretty maid," said Tom, the next line of the song coming unbidden to his lips. He held his breath and wondered what she would say.

"Nobody asked you to," she said, supplying the final line. "We were children then; our marriage does not seem a good idea now." This was easier than she thought it was going to be. She held her breath and waited for his answer.

"To be honest, I'm not ready to settle down yet, I have too much to do. It would not be fair to you to ask you to wait; it could be many years yet. And we can't go through all this again for a while," said Tom, with a smile, indicating the chaos in the inn kitchen. "If you find another man, I will not stand in your way. On the contrary, I will wish you both well." He thought she might have been upset. He was glad she wasn't, but had she never wanted him? What was wrong with him? Mary Ann had said he was a good catch.

"I've no plans to marry," said Nancy. She felt better now Tom knew where he stood, but she wondered if it had been too easy. Shouldn't he have argued with her? But usually people didn't. It almost felt as if Tom was meeting her half way.

"The cream has run out but there is lots of apple pie left," said Mary Ann as she came running in. "I wondered where you had got to, Miss."

Nancy handed the jug to Mary Ann and waited for her to go.

"I thought you said they were waiting for it," said Nancy as Mary Ann hesitated, hoping to hear more, before she finally went.

"That'll save us having to tell everybody," said Nancy.

"Once Mary Ann tells your sisters, the whole town will know about it," said Tom. "I certainly didn't fancy telling my mother; she can't wait to get us all married. I might make myself scarce for a while."

"My father likes having me home, so he won't mind," said Nancy. She was sure that Mary Ann would spread the gossip, rather than her sisters, but was not going to argue the point.

"Let's go and watch the bride and groom leave to go home," said Tom. "We don't want them slipping away quietly."

14 THE BEST MAN

The bride and groom had left for home, and Tom was happily watching Nancy reorganize the dancing. She had stationed herself between the fiddle player and the path to the ale, and was giving instructions to the dancers. Nancy wanted everything to be done properly, with each dancer following the correct path through the set.

Unfortunately, some of the dancers had two left feet at the best of times and their heavy boots did not help. There were others who meant well, but their feet were befuddled after a long day's revelry. This group started by following their natural instincts to move to the right, remembered Nancy's instructions to move to the left and then stood wondering what to do next. Clockwise, followed by anticlockwise, followed by confusion.

Nancy was getting more and more annoyed and Tom was trying to keep his face straight. The grass was getting churned up, Arthur was right about that. Tom thought he was alone, until he heard Mary Ann's voice.

"I'm glad you are not marrying Nancy."

"And why is that?" asked Tom, glad that someone in the family was going to be on his side.

"Sally and Susan say that life hasn't been much fun since Nancy got her own class at school. She's still all schoolteachery when she gets home and there is trouble when they do not obey her right away."

"That mightn't do them any harm." said Tom.

"But I wouldn't want to be related to a schoolteacher. I would never get a rest from school."

"I thought you liked school."

"It'll be better now I am going into the top class. Mr. Watson usually has a sleep after lunch to give his class a rest."

"Don't you want to be a monitor, and learn to become a teacher?"

"No thank you. I'd like to be a dressmaker like Jeannie, but there may be a bit too much sewing. It must be wonderful to make fancy hats all day."

"So you don't worry about what will become of me if I am left on the shelf?"

"Don't worry, I will look after you in your old age. I will make sure you are eating properly, and I will tidy up the shop for you. Especially that back room."

Tom thought that the world was full of women wanting to order him about. For good measure, he saw his mother in the distance; she seemed to be looking for someone.

"I'll keep mother talking, if you want to get away," said Mary Ann helpfully.

***

Tom moved inside, looking for a quiet corner. There were still two people near the remainder of the food, and he went over to join them.

"I thought that I would find you here, Charlie," said Tom.

"I am not very good at dancing, Dr. Tom, and the food is very good. I thought perhaps I could learn how to make a fruit pie for you and Dr. Jarvis. I just need to test one or two first," said Charlie.

"Have you actually moved away from the food table this evening?" asked Tom.

"I signed papers to say I must keep away from ale houses, so I thought I had better stay near the food, where it is safe. Kit's the blacksmith's new apprentice; he has to keep away from ale houses as well, so I am looking after him."

Tom hid a smile at the thought of little Charlie looking after Kit, who was twice his size.

"And what are you two supposed to be doing?"

"We are on duty; in case we are needed. You might need me to hold your bag and help to patch people up. Kit might be needed to take someone home in the wheelbarrow. Ale houses are funny places; they make men a bit unsteady on their feet."

A yell and a muffled curse was heard from outside.

"We need a doctor! Some idiot has fallen over the peg again," called Arthur.

"Well, Charlie, it looks as if you will both be needed," said Tom.

***

Tom was not surprised to find that his brother Robert was the casualty; he had fallen over the peg on the green and landed rather awkwardly. The party was beginning to break up so Charlie and Kit were dispatched to take Robert home in the wheelbarrow. Tom went inside to look for William, and found him in the saloon bar with some of the town's older men.

"Was there much damage done?" asked Arthur's father, Edward.

"The green is fine, but the patient broke his nose," said Tom.

"Did you have trouble setting it?" asked William.

"There were plenty of people to hold him down, which made it easier. He had got to the stage where he couldn't feel much pain so we didn't need to give him any brandy and I managed to set his nose fairly quickly," said Tom.

"How does he look?" asked William. "Usually they end up with a face that only a mother could love."

"Robert will keep most of his good looks, but might snore for a bit," said Tom. "I'm glad I am not sharing a room with him. He went home in the wheelbarrow before it is in demand later on."

"I hope you're not referring to us," said Richard "Us old 'uns' can hold our drink much better than today's lads."

"Years of practice," said Edward.

"Where would you be if we didn't have the occasional drink?" asked William. "You would only have the passing trade and mail delivery."

"I know we shouldn't profit by men's weaknesses," said Edward "but we all do it. What if there was no demand for laudanum or tobacco? Would you be able to keep an apprentice and two fine horses if all your money came from doctoring?"

"You have a point there," said William. "But it seems that there's more drunkenness about now, especially amongst the younger men. Always causing trouble, getting into fights."

"That keeps us in work, too!" said Tom.

"I'm sure everything was different when we were younger and everyone worked on the land," said William.

"When they worked on the land, there was no free time to go to the ale houses. They were so busy, especially in the summer," said Richard. He had worked in the area for a long time. "Life was just as hard. When the reforms come in, life will get easier."

"What reforms?" asked John, who had just come in.

"When the Tory government falls, the Whigs want to make sure that each town gets a fair share of the vote. At the moment some small villages send a member of parliament to London, and the new big towns have none. Now all the laws are in favour of the big landowners. The towns get nothing because they are not represented," said Edward.

"Will all the men have a vote, or just gentlemen like at the moment," asked Richard.

"It's hard to say. It will probably still be men, above a certain age, and above a certain income. They will argue about the limits for ages, but I don't expect they will change much," said Edward.

"Will it make any difference to us?" asked John.

"Probably not for a while, we are too far away from London," said Edward.

"How do you know all this?" asked Tom.

"All the important people pass through here on the coaches, sometimes they stay overnight. I hear all their talk," said Edward.

"Oh, there you are, Tom," said John, your mother was looking for you earlier on, she would like a little word."

"I am sorry, I have to go now, I promised to help Arthur with the quoit green," said Tom. "It's very important that we start work on it now."

"Vital," said Richard.

***

It was a clear moonlit night; the dancers were on their way home. Everything was quiet except for the mumble of the older men talking inside, the steady trundle of the wheelbarrow and an occasional retching from one of the revellers.

"These clods of earth that have been dug up are called divots. If we stamp them in straight away, the quoit green will mend quickly," said Tom.

"Like this?" asked Arthur.

"Yes, we should take our time and make sure we get all of them. The lords in the south hire staff to do this after every polo match."

"Does it always work?"

"The green will be good as new in time for the match."

"So we have nothing to blame when we lose."

"Richard said he had a talented new player."

"That's what I heard. Do you know anything about this Christopher Dawson?" asked Arthur.

"I heard he is young and strong."

"Do you know his family?"

"I don't think he has one."

"I have never seen him drinking in here," said Arthur, who thought he knew everybody.

"Probably hasn't any money,"

"Unknown penniless orphan plays the match of his life and saves the town's honour? I don't think so."

"Never in real life."

"What were they talking about before you came out?"

"Not the match. Parliamentary reform."

"My dad is always talking about things like that. Seems to me that Parliament is a lot of old men talking and not getting anything done," said Arthur.

"We don't need to go to London for that," said Tom. "We are very good at it here."

15 THE VICTIM

It was not too bad working with the gang again, and the first week was over. Benjie stood in line to collect his first week's wages from Ma, and noticed that some of the men were a bit cooler to him than they used to be. He knew that many of the men had been jealous of him when he had the chance to help look after the horses at the Queen's Arms. That was a plum job, and had gone to one of Frank's cronies last year.

Perhaps some of the men thought Benjie got special treatment because he was Ma's grandson, but they should know that was not true. And things were working more smoothly since he got back, now that he was looking after the horse and driving the cart. He moved up to the top of the line, but missed his friend Wiggy, and wished that the other men were friendlier.

Ma handed Benjie his money, only half of what he usually got. Frank was standing next to Ma, and moved to the men's side of the table.

"I think there has been a mistake, I usually get more than this," said Benjie, but he slipped his money into his pocket just in case.

"Your wages have been docked because of the extra food you gave to the horse. Feed costs money," said Ma.

"I thought Star was looking a bit peaky, and needed building up so that he could pull those heavy loads. So he could work better for you."

"Peaky he says! Your posh horses at the inn may look 'peaky' but this one is just lazy. You can't expect to keep the horse in luxury and still get paid."

"He is doing his best, but he is just a bag of bones," said Benjie, and realized that he had said too much. He should have been more careful with the extra hay as well, feeding Star when nobody was looking. Looking after horses at the Queen's Arms had been very different, and he had got used to their way of doing things.

"Don't you dare argue," said Ma. "Frank! Show the men what happens to anyone who argues with me."

Benjie did not see Frank's fist until it was too late.

***

Benjie picked himself up off the floor; he felt bruised and could taste blood in his mouth. Everyone else had gone, and so had the money in his pocket. As he slowly came to, he realized that he was on his own and needed to find an easy way of coping. Benjie had saved some money; it was still in his boot, but he needed to find somewhere to hide it as there was nowhere safe at home. He only had two relatives in Gorton, so it had to be Charlie. Risky, but he would rather Charlie spent the money than Frank and his cronies.

Benjie felt a bit wobbly as walked up the road, but the feeling passed. His mouth was a bit painful; perhaps he would ask Mr. Tom to have a look and see if any more teeth needed pulling.

When Benjie arrived at the shop, Charlie was working hard with a mortar and pestle and Tom was supervising.

"Always keep busy when you are in the shop, and come and ask me if you run out of things to do," said Tom. "It gives a good impression to the customers. That powder looks right now; you can start work on the shelves".

Charlie set about the shelves with enthusiasm, but Benjie managed to avoid the clouds of dust as he came through the door.

"You've been in the wars," said Tom. "I won't ask what happened. I had better take a look at the damage."

"A few bruises, they will heal. This front tooth is wobbly; will it have to come out?" asked Benjie.

"I'll have a look. I may be able to bed the tooth back in. What happened to the other front tooth?"

"It must have been knocked out," said Benjie after he searched with his tongue and found the gap.

"Do you have it with you?"

"Didn't think. You can't put it back in, can you?"

"I could try, but no promises."

"I'll go and see if I can find it."

"No, Charlie can go if you tell him where you think it is. Charlie, take a glass of milk to put the tooth in, don't you dare put it in that dirty pocket of yours," said Tom. Charlie rushed off after instructions from Benjie.

"This other tooth should bed in if you are careful. Can you just hold it in place while I clean up the gap?"

"Have you done this very often before?"

"No, to be honest, but I have watched it being done. Lot of fights in

Edinburgh, but the lads still wanted to look their best. I always wanted to have a go at this, if you don't mind being my first patient. I won't charge, in case it doesn't work."

Benjie sat still and silent as Tom worked away, but he looked a little grey around the gills. After a while Charlie came back with the missing tooth.

"Can you really stick it back in?" asked Charlie.

"I'll have a go. It is in one piece, and came out recently, so it is worth trying. Benjie knows that it might not work, but we have nothing to lose."

"Now Benjie, this will take time, and you won't be able to talk for a while. Would you like us to send a message to your grandmother, to let her know that you have been hurt and will be back later than expected?" asked Tom.

Benjie thought for a while. His gran knew fine well that he had been hurt and none of the men were expected back from the ale house until late. Then he remembered where he had planned to go that evening.

"I was hoping to go to Miss Graham for my writing lesson; she will be expecting me. Perhaps if she knew I wasn't coming, she could get on with something more important."

"Off you go, Charlie, just tell Miss Graham that Benjie had a mishap and won't be coming. Don't dwell on the injuries, women are squeamish about such things. Right, here we go. Hopefully it will work. Wave your hands if you want me to stop for a bit. Pity it wasn't a broken nose, I am quite good with those now, and my last patient looked almost passable," said Tom.

Benjie sat in enforced silence, trying not to move as Tom worked.

***

Tom had finished the work by the time Charlie slunk quietly back in.

"You were quick, I thought you would have stayed to talk to Kit. Did you deliver the message?" asked Tom.

"Yes, but Miss Graham was ever so funny about it. I think she wanted to rush down and see if Benjie was all right, but the blacksmith talked her out of it. She asked me lots of questions about what happened," said Charlie.

"And?" asked Tom.

"I couldn't tell her, because I wasn't there, but she kept on. And then I got lots of questions about the injuries. I wouldn't like to be in her class, Dr. Tom. She has ways of getting the truth out of a lad, you wouldn't believe. And I have heard about how she uses her cane..."

Benjie couldn't believe what Charlie was saying. The lovely Miss Graham forcing information out of Charlie? Owning a cane? Using it on the children at school? Never! He waved his hands as if he wanted to protest, but Tom asked him to be still and let his teeth settle. Tom looked as if he was hiding a smile.

"Were there any messages, or did you rush away too quickly?" asked Tom.

"Mr. Graham asked about the quoit green," said Charlie.

"Good as new," said Tom.

"Oh, and Miss Graham said she hoped to see Benjie next week, if he is well enough," said Charlie.

Benjie was delighted and couldn't help breaking out into a smile.

"You really did stick the tooth back in," said Charlie," I wish I had been able to watch."

"Maybe next time," said Tom. "Then you can watch and learn."

"If other bits fall off a man, can you put them back on? Could we mend a man from spare parts, like mending a cart?" asked Charlie.

"Nails and hair grow again, wounds can be stitched and bones can be set," said Tom. "But limbs can't be replaced. And they can't grow again like a lizard's tail. So forget about building people from spare parts, it will never happen."

"So we couldn't build a monster in the cellar?" asked Charlie. Benjie tried not to laugh.

"Definitely not, we haven't room because of all the junk," said Tom.

"And I was just going to see if we had a space!" said Charlie.

They were all so amused by the thought of the monster in the cellar, that they did not notice Arthur come in.

"I've an urgent letter for you, Tom, came in the last mail coach. I thought I had better bring it across myself, as all the servants are busy serving ale," said Arthur. "I could wait and see if there is a reply. I hope your family are all right."

The letter was marked "Urgent" and "Secret" and Tom could see that Arthur and Charlie wanted to know what was in it. He recognized the writing, and letters from this direction were very few and far between.

"That's all right, no need for you to wait."

"If you are sure," said Arthur, hovering.

"Charlie, I would like you to stay with Benjie for a while, Dr. Jarvis has just come back from work in the infirmary, and I would like to talk to him about the patients," said Tom, and he went through to the back, taking the letter with him.

This gave Benjie a chance to explain his real errand; he wanted to leave his little bit of money with Charlie for safety. Benjie hoped Charlie would look after the money and not spend it on one of his own little projects.

***

The following week, Benjie stayed out of trouble. His bruises had faded, and both front teeth were surprisingly firm. Benjie slipped away discreetly when the gang went to the ale house, and set off towards the blacksmith's. He thought it sensible to go the long way, and tidied himself up a bit when nobody was looking.

His mind was in turmoil; he couldn't think why he was so excited. But Miss

Graham had asked Charlie about his injuries! She asked to see him this week! Someone as important and wonderful and lovely as Nancy actually wanted to see him! He knocked on the door; the blacksmith let him in and went back to the forge. Nancy was standing inside on her own, no sign of her sisters.

"Sorry about last week, Miss Graham. I had a bit of an accident."

"Charlie explained. You had all those terrible injuries, and lost all that blood. You were very brave!"

"It wasn't quite like that, Miss Graham."

"Call me Nancy."

16 THE UNDERSTANDING

Nancy just stood there, looking at Benjie; she was so glad to see him in one piece. From the information she dragged out of Charlie, Benjie had sustained some nasty injuries the previous week. Sally had heard rumours that Benjie had been badly beaten up and had all his teeth knocked out, but he seemed to have a full set of teeth. Susan was telling everyone that Benjie had been at death's door, and that the surgeon had miraculously cured him.

"I'm so glad you are all right, I'd heard that you had been hurt," said Nancy softly, as she walked towards him.

"Sound as a bell, but didn't Charlie say there was nothing seriously wrong?" asked Benjie.

"Yes, he did, but I've heard all sorts of rumours since then," said Nancy. She looked for her sisters but remembered that they were out. She would have a word with them later, but was not looking forward to it as much as she usually did, even though she had been badly frightened.

"You can see for yourself that I am fine," said Benjie, smiling. His front tooth was a bit chipped; she couldn't remember if it had always been like that.

"I was so worried," said Nancy. "How did it all happen? I heard lots of conflicting accounts."

"I really can't remember, and nobody seemed to see what happened. I must have fallen," said Benjie. He could not admit that he was having problems at work. "You shouldn't worry about the likes of me, I am only a farm hand."

"I could have lost you," said Nancy, putting her hand on his arm to make sure that he was really there. She felt the thrill of touching him, just like she had when they first met. She couldn't quite believe what was happening; she had never felt like this with Tom. She supposed it must be how Jeannie felt with George, and a whole new world seemed to beckon.

"You can always get another pupil."

"I couldn't replace you." Nancy's hand was still on his arm and neither of them had made any attempt to move.

"It doesn't matter about the likes of me."

"I was so worried." Her lower lip quivered and Benjie put his arm around her. She felt warm and protected and safe. She had never expected any man to give her this feeling. She had thought that men were stupid great lummocks that had to be managed for their own good, until now.

"You are a lady, Miss Graham, you shouldn't get upset about what happens to a lowly farm hand," said Benjie. But they still did not move.

"Call me Nancy," she said, moving closer for a kiss.

***

They made no attempt to open any of the books that evening. Benjie and Nancy were content to just be with each other. Nancy was sitting on Benjie's lap and did not want to be anywhere else. They said very little, in case it broke the spell. They forgot about the outside world, and were startled when someone came in.

Benjie tried to struggle to his feet, but Nancy kept him firmly in his place.

"I see you have Benjie pinned down," said Richard "so that you can have your wicked way with him. I hope your intentions are honourable."

"Sorry, Mr. Graham, I wouldn't presume, but…" said Benjie.

"I insisted," said Nancy.

"I'm asking your permission to court Miss Graham," said Benjie.

"Call me Nancy," she said. She would normally have shouted at this stage, but she couldn't shout at Benjie.

"I'd understand if you said no, I have nothing to offer her. Nancy is a fine lady, too good for the likes of me. She could have anyone she wanted," said Benjie.

"You have my blessing," said Richard, as the cloud on his horizon lifted. Although there was nothing he could put his finger on, he imagined that home life would be more comfortable with just his other two daughters at home. Richard didn't want to rush anything, but he hoped the marriage would be soon. He liked Benjie and thought that Nancy would find him more biddable than Tom.

"I really have your blessing? But I am not good enough…" started Benjie.

"What about your own family?" asked Richard.

"I don't think I would get my grandmother's blessing, so there is no point asking for it. She is dead set against me bettering myself," said Benjie. "I need Dr. Tom's blessing. It wouldn't be right otherwise. I will speak to him as soon as possible. And he ought to be the first to know, not find it out from his sister, Mary Ann."

"I don't think that is really necessary," said Nancy, but she wasn't going to argue.

"I must go now, before I am missed," said Benjie. "I will come back when I have spoken to Dr. Tom."

When Sally and Susan came back a few minutes later they found their father particularly cheerful; they supposed the preparations for the quoits match had been going well. Nancy seemed to be in a world of her own, and did not pay much attention to their amazing piece of gossip.

"I saw Dr. Tom get on to the mail coach, and he had his bag with him," said Sally.

"He must be out on a visit," said Nancy.

"He usually rides that horse of his," said Susan. "Mary Ann says he likes to show off. He must be going quite a long way; don't you wonder where he is going?"

"I have no idea," said Nancy.

"Mary Ann didn't know either," said Sally. "There must be some big secret."

"It's not our concern," said Nancy.

***

Nancy found that the next few days went very slowly with no word or visit from Benjie. She wondered if he stayed away out of respect for Tom's feelings, or possibly because he had changed his mind, and did not love her. In Nancy's lighter moments, she knew that Benjie was kept busy and was not likely to get an opportunity to see her until the next pay day, when the rest of the gang were in the ale house.

In her darker moments, she imagined all sorts of possibilities. Benjie could have had an accident, and be maimed or even worse. Perhaps he had been injured and was lying in a ditch, miles from anywhere, crying for help. He could be already dead, lost forever. These thoughts kept her awake in the middle of the night, but in the morning she always realized that nothing of the sort could happen in Gorton without everyone knowing. Mary Ann was such a gossip, she heard everything and always made sure that Sally and Susan were kept informed.

Nancy pulled herself together; she did not want her sisters to know about her feelings for Benjie. It was early days, and might come to nothing. Just suppose Sally dropped a tiny hint to Mary Ann – the news would be all around the town in no time. More importantly, the news would be all around the school and she did not want the whisperings undermining her authority.

Nancy tried to plan for the start of the school year; there were going to be a few changes. Her older pupils would go to Mr. Watson's class and he would undo all the good work she had been doing. Adam was due to start as a pupil teacher; he was young and keen. The other teachers wanted to divide the classes so that Adam had his own pupils, but Nancy put her foot down. She insisted on hanging on to her own allotted age range; she thought that Adam would have trouble controlling a class as he had been a pupil so recently.

Nancy said that Adam should help Mr. Watson with his class. Mr. Watson was getting too old and tired to argue with Nancy, and Mrs. Hull was told that juniors were not her concern. In the end it was decided that Adam could help Nancy as well, but she was quite sure that she didn't need any help. Mrs. Hull's older pupils were to be promoted to Nancy's class - they would have a lot of catching up to do - and Nancy would have to find little jobs for Adam to do as well. And she had promised Tom that Charlie could attend school in the mornings. She would have liked to teach Charlie herself, but realized that he was too old for her class. Charlie had been out of school for a long time, so someone needed to keep an eye on him and she was not sure that Mr. Watson was capable of it.

Unless Nancy made sure that the children behaved themselves and learnt properly, everything would descend into chaos, nobody would employ the children and they would all end up in the poorhouse.

Usually Nancy had a lot of satisfaction when she considered her place in the order of things, but she still felt very restless. Her sisters were looking at her a bit strangely, so she decided to keep them busy with a spring clean.

"We already had a spring clean this year," said Sally.

"The house looks dirty, it all needs cleaning again," said Nancy "You can start by taking up the rugs and beating them on the clothesline."

"I'm sure they do not need it," said Sally.

"Do as you are told, said Nancy. She climbed on to a stool to reach the curtains, and just caught sight of Susan going out of the door." Where do you think you are sneaking off to, Miss Susan?"

"Mary Ann is expecting me," said Susan.

"She will have to wait. I want you to make a start on the kitchen now!" said Nancy as she took down the curtains and bustled off towards the wash house at the back of the house. "I'll be watching you, so no slacking."

"We did all this in March," said Susan. "Surely it can wait a bit longer. It is a lovely day out there."

"A lovely day for drying washing!" said Nancy. "All the bedding needs airing as well. No time to stand about."

"All this because Dr. Tom disappeared into a mail coach and didn't tell you where he was going," said Susan.

Nancy's face was like thunder and she took a deliberate step towards her sister. Susan squeaked and ran into the kitchen.

Nancy was sure that Tom did not make any difference to her life anymore, but she wondered why he went off so suddenly.

17 THE SHOTGUN

Tom wanted to look at this strange new place, but he could see nothing out of the windows because of the all-pervading grey mist. Not a gentle drizzle, like at home, or a fog like Edinburgh sometimes had, but a cold, damp grey mist that got worse as he got nearer to the coast.

Tom looked for his doctor's bag, less likely to get lost inside the carriage than with other people's luggage outside. When he left home, people would have thought that he had been called out on a visit somewhere. And if highwaymen attacked, they were less likely to harm a doctor in case they needed him later. Highwaymen! What sort of a place was he coming to?

The other passengers seemed to have slowly melted away, Tom was the only one left in the eerie silence. He read the letter again, and thought carefully about the contents.

Dear Tom

I am in a fix and need your help. No surprises. *I got a Darlington girl into trouble, it wasn't my fault honest, she led me on.* It takes two. *Her father wants us to get married, and her big brothers want to rearrange my face for me.* Brothers can be very protective. *That would be a shame as you went to all that trouble to fix my nose.* I don't want my work ruined.

I need you to come as soon as you can, but please can you make sure that mother doesn't know until the wedding is over. That is tricky, it meant avoiding the gossips; if mother finds out from Mary Ann she will be livid. *I will need father's consent, as I am under age, perhaps you could explain and get him to sign something when he comes to your shop for his tobacco.* Father will let the truth slip, hopefully before I get back. If Robert thinks it is not a good idea for mother to go to the wedding, he probably has a good reason. But I don't want to be the one to tell her.

Please come. I really need someone from my family, as there will be so many of Bridget's. That last line got me. I will do what I can.

Your brother

Robert

They must be near the coast now; he could still see nothing but could hear seagulls. Tom was glad that the uncomfortable journey was nearly over; he had felt every stone and pothole in the road.

***

Tom stepped out of the coach into a different world. He could see nothing clearly and the air felt very damp and cold considering the season. The people around him were talking a strange language; the rhythm was very different from what he was used to. Hammer, hammer, hammer all the way rapidly up and down the scale, consonants very pronounced. Tom noticed the rhythm because he couldn't make out a single spoken word.

The coachman was talking to him, and he just couldn't understand what he was saying. Tom could understand the Scots in Edinburgh but these people seemed to be from a different country. He needed a friendly, English speaking native. Fast.

Robert stepped out of the mist.

"What's he saying?" asked Tom.

"He hopes this is where you meant to meet your brother off the coach because it is the end of the line," said Robert.

Tom looked around; it looked like the end of the line. It looked like the end of the world!

"How did you know I was on this coach?"

"I met every coach for the last two days, I am so glad you could come. Joe is in Hilltop and I couldn't drag George away from his new wife."

"I wanted a change of scene. William said I had been working too hard." Be careful what you wish for. "Do you really like living here? Once you get married and settle down, there is no going back." Tom could hear women yammering away like fishwives; they sounded hard. As they walked along towards Robert's lodgings, he wondered what his younger brother had got himself into.

"The work is exciting, part of something really new. We will all be travelling by rail and will be able to go wherever we like – and I am making it possible. Plate by plate by plate."

Tom wondered if the railway would be more comfortable than the coach. Definitely not as biddable as Thunderbolt, and it would have to stay on the track.

"The railway will never replace the canal or the horse and cart."

"It will be a whole different world."

Tom preferred the world he was used to.

"If you are not sure about living and working here, we can still go home."

"I wouldn't want to be stuck in the mill like George, or be out in all that Hilltop weather like Joe."

"I think Joe spends more time brewing than labouring these days."

"And I wouldn't want to be called out at night like you. I like to finish my work at the end of the day, and then go home to Bridget. Regular hours, a good dinner and a comfortable bed. A wife to look after me would make it perfect."

Tom loved his work, and would not like regular hours at all. He loved the thrill of being called out at night and sometimes things took longer than expected. Tom would not like to be hampered by the thought of a bad tempered wife at home, tapping her foot and waiting for him to come in.

"I lodge with the Murphys, Bridget's mam and dad. The Irish community have been very good to me; some are miners, some work on the railway," said Robert. "Just around this corner. Did you bring dad's letter?"

"Yes, but we could still say that he withheld his consent if you like. You are very young to tie yourself down. Are you sure the baby is yours?"

"Bridget is not the type to shake a loose leg. I love her; she is a canny lass."

Tom thought that perhaps Robert would do well with a steady girl who was careful with money, and bowed to the inevitable.

***

Bridget had brown curly hair, freckles, a ready smile and laughing eyes. Mrs. Murphy looked like Bridget but her hair was grey, the freckles faded, and her face was old and tired, but her eyes still twinkled in spite of it all. Mr. Murphy had just come in from the pit, he was coughing and his face was black. They looked much older than Tom's parents - what did this place do to people? Would Bridget look like her mother in twenty years' time?

Mr. Murphy sent Robert to fetch the coal while the women made dinner, so that he could have a 'man to man' talk with Tom.

"Robert tells me you are a doctor."

"Surgeon and apothecary. I served an apprenticeship."

"So you understand the ways of the world."

"More or less."

"I don't want to force Robert to get married, but someone needs to provide for Bridget and the bairn. Otherwise they could starve when we have gone."

"Robert is under age, but knows his own mind."

"We've got fond of him, he's a canny lad."

Tom disagreed but didn't say anything. Robert let money go through his hands like water.

"If he didn't want to marry, I wouldn't force him as long as he looked after them. But Bridget's brothers are fretting; she is their only sister and they are very protective. You know how it is."

"Yes I do. Robert and I have two younger sisters; one of them is still at school. The other one is poorly and I am quite worried about her." Tom had taken action when his parents had not thought it necessary; brothers had a better idea about how to keep their sisters safe.

After dinner, there was a loud knock on the door.

"That will be the lads," said Mrs. Murphy proudly.

Three large men loomed in the doorway.

"We have come for Robert," said the largest.

Robert stood up, and Tom stood up with him. He hoped there was no fighting but was quite prepared to defend his brother.

"Where are you taking him?" asked Tom.

"To the ale house," said the youngest," a man needs a drink on his last night of freedom."

The third brother had twinkling eyes like his mother and sister.

"Howay man," he said, "the beer is getting cold."

"Get off with you," said Mr. Murphy. "My only daughter is getting married tomorrow; I need to get the bath out".

***

Tom knew they had a good evening; he wished he could remember all of it. A very friendly ale house, with music and singing that went on well into the night. There were fiddles, pipes, an accordion and a strange looking drum that all made the evening go with a swing. Even Tom and Robert were singing; they couldn't carry a tune in a bucket but it didn't seem to matter.

It had been a mistake to try and match Bridget's brothers drink for drink, he knew that now, but it only seemed polite at the time. He thought he could remember dancing a jig; that couldn't be right. He could remember Robert climbing on to the table and he could remember Robert falling off the table. He could remember them setting everything to rights again, and the giggling, while other people didn't seem to notice and just carried on with the music. It was the bits in between that he wasn't sure about.

They had come back a different way because someone wanted to show them some canny leeks in the back yard, but he couldn't remember what they looked like. It seemed to take ages to get back, and then they were falling over and giggling and trying not to wake Bridget and her parents. And his head hurt.

There was a loud groan from Robert in the bed next to him.

"I feel terrible, I must be dying," said Robert.

"Hurry up and get dressed, you have a big day today," said Tom.

"What's happening?"

"You are marrying Bridget."

"I'm poorly, I want me mam."

"You don't want to disappoint Bridget and her nice brothers, do you?"

"Have you got any medicine in that bag of yours?"

Tom produced a brandy flask, drank a little for good measure, and passed it to his brother. Robert took a sip and his eyes lit up.

"This is good medicine," said Robert as he took a hefty swig. He reached for it again but Tom had put it back in the bag. Robert said that he felt a lot better, but Tom noticed that he was a little unsteady on his feet.

***

The wedding took place as planned and everybody heaved a sigh of relief. Robert was swaying a little, so Tom had to support him on the way up to the altar. Bridget kept a firm grip on him after that, trying to keep a straight face as she said her vows. The church was new, and rather hurriedly put together; it seemed to be made out of wood. Tom thought it was very different from the old church at home but it did its job well enough.

They went back to the Murphys' afterwards; more friends and relatives arrived to wish them well.

"Where will you live?" asked Tom.

"I hadn't thought. I suppose I will share Bridget's attic," said Robert.

"The attic might be a bit small for the three of you." said Mrs. Murphy.

"There's a little back to back house just around the corner," said Mr. Murphy. "You earn good money as a platelayer, you wouldn't have a problem with the rent."

"Are you trying to get rid of us?" asked Bridget, "and replace us with more lodgers?"

"Of course not! said her mother. "What would you need?"

"A bed," said Robert.

"Sure isn't that what got us into trouble in the first place!" said Bridget.

"You could have old man Reagan's bed now the wake and funeral is over," said Mrs. Murphy.

"It is a good bed. He was born, bedded his wife, died and was laid out in that bed. Built to last, a good few years in it yet," said Mr. Murphy.

"Perhaps you don't fancy having a bed that a man died in so recently," said Tom. Jeannie would have been picky about it and Nancy would have definitely refused.

Robert opened his mouth to say something, but Bridget was there first.

"Sure, the old man won't be needing it any more, will he?" she said.

The wedding breakfast descended into chaos as four men rushed off to get the bed, and people fetched bedding, plates, spoons and pans to tide the newlyweds over until Bridget could get to the market or the pawnshop. It seemed very haphazard, but the youngsters were enjoying 'playing house' and the Murphys were asking around about possible lodgers. Tom left Robert some money for a wedding present, and went back on the next coach.

***

William was sitting with his pipe and drop of brandy when Tom got back.

"Has everything been all right here?"

"Fairly quiet, Charlie and I managed fine."

"It won't be so easy when Charlie is at school in the mornings next week. We will have to fend for ourselves. Were there any messages for me?"

"Your mother called in. She seemed a bit put out."

"I saw George when I got off the coach, so I can delay my visit home for a day or two. "Anyone else?"

"Benjie Armstrong called."

80

"To see Charlie?"

"To see you."

"I wonder what he wanted."

"I don't know. He said he'd call back next week," said William.

18 THE BLESSING

Benjie was having a very difficult week, Star was very bad tempered and so was Frank. Benjie found it very difficult to prevent Frank beating the horse and it was even more difficult to prevent Star from kicking Frank, knowing that Benjie would get the blame. Benjie could not find anything physically wrong with Star, and Ma Armstrong thought that it would be a waste of money to ask for advice. Perhaps Star had just taken a scunner for some reason; he certainly had cause to bear a grudge.

It all came to a head when all the gang was gathered for breakfast, after working in the fields for four hours.

"Lots of work to do today, so don't even think of skiving off to see one of your fancy horse doctors," said Frank.

"I'd like to have him checked if possible, he would work much better," said Benjie. "If we're so busy, it could wait."

"It can wait for ever," said Frank. "That horse needs to know who is boss." Benjie thought that Star knew who was boss, and just didn't like him. Maybe he would ask the blacksmith for advice next time Star needed shoes; it would give him an excuse to spend more time there.

"You've no time for chatting, I need some supplies from town. Benjie, since you have obviously finished your breakfast, get the horse and cart ready," said Ma Armstrong. "I need you, Frank, and your brother Ox." Ox was even bigger than Frank, but a little slow on the uptake.

"The men won't work if I don't stand over them," said Frank. "Can't Ox and Benjie manage?"

"I have a little business to do in town as well, I may need your help," said Ma.

***

Once Ma had haggled over prices, she and Frank sat on the cart while

Benjie and Ox carried the heavy sacks. Ma seemed to be looking up and down the street for someone.

"It's my favourite grandson!" said Ma. Benjie knew that she didn't mean him. "Charlie! I wondered what had happened to you!"

Charlie was out doing errands; he looked at the cart in surprise and smiled when he saw Benjie.

"What are you doing?"

"I am working for the doctors."

"A young lad like you shouldn't be working so hard, you should be out playing. You come and stay with your nice gran and good for nothing cousin, and you will be looked after properly."

"Run, Charlie," shouted Benjie before Frank 'pole axed' him.

He looked up to find Ma holding Charlie firmly by the ear, and Frank looming over him. Charlie started yelling, making as much noise as he could to attract attention; a large crowd was gathering and William stepped forward.

"What do you think you are doing with my apprentice," said William.

"I'm taking my grandson home, I am his legal guardian and no-one can do anything about it," said Ma.

"Dr. Harrison and I are Charlie's legal guardians; he was signed over to us from the poorhouse. Charlie belongs to us until his apprenticeship is over and we have put a lot of time and money into his training," said William.

"I don't believe you," said Ma but she relaxed her grip on Charlie's ear. He would have broken loose but Frank still held his arm in a firm grip. Charlie started yelling again as he realized he needed to keep the crowd's attention.

"We have the papers signed and sealed. Dr. Harrison has gone to fetch the magistrate; he foresaw that there might be a little difficulty."

"That is wicked, taking a little boy away from his family. Don't you want to come home, Charlie?"

Charlie looked at the supplies on the cart, and compared them to the food he ate at the doctors' house.

"No," said Charlie, correcting it to "No, thank you", after a look from William.

They would have all been standing there all day if Tom had not arrived with the magistrate.

"Charlie Armstrong is the property of Dr. Jarvis and Dr. Harrison. Anyone who takes him away or interferes in any way is committing a criminal offence and could go to jail," said the magistrate.

Ma thought about the jail, nicknamed the jug because people had been dropped in from the top of the building in previous times.

"I just wanted to see my poor little grandson, sent away into child slavery. When the apprenticeship is over, he can come home to his gran and have a rest. How old will he be then?" asked Ma.

"Twenty-one, and a qualified doctor. He will not need a guardian, and will be able to choose where he lives," said Tom.

Ma knew they were outnumbered; she, Frank and Ox got back on the cart as the crowd watched.

"Why are you sitting there gawping, Benjie, drive this cart home," said Ma.

Benjie was still a little dazed. Ox had to prop him up as he picked up the reins.

"Charlie, you can come and see your family if ever they give you any free time," said Ma.

Benjie knew that Charlie would not be making that journey, and tried to hide a smile of triumph.

***

Benjie had two days mucking out the pigs on top of his normal duties. His pay was reduced again, but he knew better than to argue. He was not looking forward to meeting Tom, as he felt he owed him several favours that he could never pay back.

"How's Charlie?" asked Benjie.

"Full of himself as ever with all the extra attention. Though he considers himself to be 'his own man' and nobody's property! Did you ever hear the like!" said Tom with a smile.

"Is he in?"

"You just missed him, he has gone to the forge to encourage Kit Dawson to throw horseshoes over a peg outside. Charlie gets a bit of time off sometimes, we don't make him work all the time in spite of what his relatives might think."

"I'm really grateful for you and Dr. Jarvis looking after Charlie," said Benjie, "but it was really you I came to see."

"Are the teeth still all right? Any more injuries to patch up?"

"I'm very grateful to you for that as well, Dr. Tom. It doesn't hurt to eat any more."

"Smile still working its magic?"

"In a manner of speaking. This is difficult, as I am beholden to you, and this is not an easy thing to say."

Tom wondered what was coming next.

"I heard that you aren't courting Miss Graham anymore," said Benjie, slowly.

"We realized we weren't really suited," said Tom, thinking of all the reasons why he didn't want to marry Nancy.

"Would it worry you if anyone else wanted to court Miss Graham?"

"He'd have my blessing. Who is the happy man?" asked Tom. He felt as if a great weight has lifted off his shoulders.

"I'd be the happiest man in the world," said Benjie, blushing. "But I am beholden to you, I don't want to take your girl".

"Nancy is free to have whoever she wants, and I want her to be happy," said Tom. "But, just between ourselves, don't you find her a bit, well, sort of…"

"I'm used to women telling me what to do," said Benjie "I wouldn't get anything done otherwise."

"But you wouldn't have much control over your life. I am really keen for you to court Nancy, but you should know that she can be a bit, well, 'managing'."

"I would love to be managed by Miss Nancy. Not that I am good enough for her, mind," said Benjie. He didn't say that she had taken the decision herself.

"I am really delighted about you and Nancy," said Tom. "I could be the best man at your wedding, I have had a lot of practice recently."

***

When Benjie got to the blacksmith's there was a crowd outside, watching Kit throw his horseshoes and enjoying Charlie's running commentary. Nobody saw Nancy opening the door to let Benjie in.

"Did you see Tom?"

"Yes, just now."

"What did he say?" asked Nancy, shouting over the noise of the crowd outside.

"He had been to see his brother in Darlington."

"No, what did he say about us?"

"We have his blessing."

"Did you have to persuade him?"

There was another roar from the crowd.

"No, he was really pleased for us, he wishes us well."

"It is a bit noisy to talk here," said Nancy, as she did not think she could have heard Benjie correctly. Surely Tom would have been a bit more reluctant?

"Do you know anywhere quieter?" asked Benjie.

"I know just the place," said Nancy, as she led him to the hayloft at the back of the house.

***

The hayloft was small, so they ended up very close together. The talking slowed down as Nancy started unbuttoning Benjie's shirt.

"What are you doing, Miss Nancy?"

"I am trying to have my wicked way with you, but you aren't helping much."

"Are you sure this is right?" asked Benjie as he helpfully took off his shirt before it got torn.

"We're courting, aren't we?" said Nancy.

"Yes, but…" said Benjie as he hesitated, wearing just his smallclothes.

"I accept your proposal of marriage," said Nancy as she rapidly undressed. "Now get those smallclothes off."

"Yes, miss," said Benjie.

"And no impertinence or I will fetch my cane," said Nancy, playfully.

"Ooh, miss," said Benjie as he allowed himself to be seduced.

***

It was getting late when Nancy and Benjie emerged from the hayloft. The crowd had gone and the children had gone to bed. Richard was sitting up, waiting.

"When you have both taken the hay out of your clothes, and Benjie has fetched his cap from the hayloft, I would like to have a little talk," said Richard.

19 THE ENGAGEMENT

Nancy was a little quieter when they faced her father, but she felt as if she was on top of the world. If this is what love is all about, it is well worth the fuss, she thought. The look on her face told all.

"Benjie and I, "she started, but her father looked at Benjie.

"I have come to ask you for your daughter's hand in marriage. But I would understand if you turned me down. I have nothing to offer her except love, and feel sure she deserves someone better," said Benjie.

"You have my permission and my blessing," said Richard. "When are you planning to marry?"

"I'd like to be married soon," said Nancy.

"Isn't that rushing it a bit?" asked Richard, hopefully.

"I would love to marry Miss Nancy as soon as possible, but I am under age and my grandmother will not give me permission to marry. She says she has spent money feeding me and clothing me for years and wants something back. That is why I don't get paid much, because of my keep," said Benjie.

"Did you know this, Nancy?" asked Richard.

"Yes, I knew. I don't care, I still want to marry Benjie as soon as possible," said Nancy.

"I think it will be better for you to wait, it is less than two years after all. Does your grandmother know who you are planning to marry?" asked Richard.

"No," said Benjie, "as it wouldn't have made any difference. And some of the men are very ignorant, and would have been saying things about Miss

Nancy and I couldn't stand that."

"What would you do if they did say things?" asked Nancy.

"I would answer them with my fists," said Benjie.

"I think that would get you into more trouble," said Richard. "I think we should keep the engagement quiet for as long as possible."

"I suppose so, but I wanted to tell the world like Jeannie did," said Nancy, although she did not want Benjie to be in any sort of danger.

"I don't mind trouble for myself, but I don't want to hurt your reputation, you being a schoolmistress and everything," said Benjie.

"Isn't he wonderful!" said Nancy.

"And if I wait until I am twenty-one, I will be able to earn a man's wage as a farm hand or even an ostler and I will have more to offer," said Benjie "Though it will not be as much as Miss Nancy has been used to."

"I would gladly wander the world with you like a gypsy," said Nancy.

"It won't come to that," said Richard. "I was thinking of setting up a carting business and was looking for an honest man to run it for me."

"That would be more than I could possibly hope for," said Benjie.

Nancy thought that being a carter's wife was not as romantic as being a gypsy, but would be a lot more comfortable, especially in winter. She could only foresee one potential problem, and didn't know how to put it delicately.

"What happens if the wedding has to be brought forward, for some reason?" she asked, innocently.

Benjie admired Nancy for thinking of everything, even though she was more forward than most girls.

"If Nancy needed the wedding to be brought forward, then we could get permission from the magistrates. But then the reason would be made public and you might not like that," said Richard.

Benjie resolved to be careful, and take a little more control, if Nancy would allow it.

"We could run off to Gretna Green," said Nancy, who quite fancied some excitement.

"I hope it doesn't come to that, "said Richard. "Elopements are very inconvenient and you couldn't have a fancy wedding like Jeannie's."

"I suppose not," said Nancy "but we could bear it in mind."

***

As the three of them discussed the future, they heard a sound on the stairs. Richard quietly opened the door to the staircase, and Sally and Susan fell into the room.

"Have you been listening at the door?" asked Richard.

"No, of course not, father," said Susan. "But isn't it exciting that Nancy is to be married to Benjie!"

"We were worried in case she was going to be left on the shelf," said Sally.

Nancy felt sure she would never have been left on the shelf. Her sisters made it sound as if she was desperate, but she had been waiting for the right man.

"It's going to be very difficult to keep the news of this engagement to ourselves now," said Richard.

"But we won't tell anyone if you don't want us to," said Susan.

"Only Mary Ann," said Sally.

"We are really good at keeping secrets," said Susan.

"Only telling one person," said Sally.

"If you tell one person, and she tells one person, and they tell one person, it will be all around the town in no time," said Richard.

"I suppose so," said Susan.

"But I am sure that Mary Ann would never tell," said Sally.

Richard put his head in his hands. "It's impossible!" he said.

"If my grandmother finds out, she may send me far away to work. To sea or even to the quarry," said Benjie. "I may never see Nancy again."

Nancy thought of giving in to her tears, but decided that it might not help to appeal to their better natures.

"If I can't marry Benjie, I won't marry anyone. I will teach at the school and live here for ever and ever," said Nancy, trying to be matter of fact and not too dramatic.

Susan and Sally thought this over. Nancy was teaching in school all day, and in the house when they got home. They loved her, as she had brought them up when their mother died. But they thought that Nancy might like a rest from her sisters sometimes and they didn't want any harm to come to Benjie.

"We could end up as three cross old maids," said Sally.

Richard shuddered.

"Tell us what you want us to do," said Susan.

"Just say nothing to anyone about Nancy's plans for the future, or about Benjie, don't even tell Mary Ann. Especially don't tell Mary Ann; don't let anything slip out. We must keep the engagement secret for as long as possible," said Richard.

"We will do as you say, father. But what if people guess, or ask us what is happening?" said Susan.

"Can we make something up?" asked Sally.

"I am not asking you to lie," said Richard "But you can say that you don't know and change the subject."

"So the secret will stay safe with the five of us," said Nancy.

"There is someone that I need to tell," said Benjie. "Dr. Tom needs to know from me, rather than from the town gossip."

"But there won't be any gossip because we won't say anything," said Susan,

"But what if he tells his sister?" asked Sally.

"Dr. Tom is not allowed to tell his patient's secrets," replied Nancy. "He swore an oath not to."

"Is that right?" asked Benjie. "I am his patient, he fixed my tooth."

"He never told Mary Ann why he wanted their sister Elizabeth to live at Hilltop for a while," said Susan.

"She writes home to say she is having a lovely time, and hardly coughs at all," added Sally.

"I always wondered about that," said Nancy.

"I had better go now if I am to catch Dr. Tom," said Benjie.

Nancy found his cap, and let him out at the back door.

"Sally and Susan, be very quiet when you go back to bed and don't wake Kit," ordered Richard.

"Why is he so important?" asked Susan.

"He needs lots of rest before Saturday," answered Richard.

Sally and Susan did not see why, but went off very quietly with no giggling.

***

Nancy went to bed, bubbling with excitement. How her life had changed in the last few hours! She had woken up as a girl, but was going to bed as a woman. She was going to marry Benjie; it was a pity that they had to wait nearly two years, but it couldn't be helped. She hoped that nothing would go wrong.

20 THE MATCH

Tom was surprised when Benjie came back to see him. He guessed that there had been further developments as soon as he saw a big smile on Benjie's face and a little hay on his clothes, but Benjie told him about it anyway.

"I told you earlier that you had my blessing, but I did not expect you to be such a quick worker," said Tom.

"Thing is, we don't want the engagement to be general knowledge yet, as I am not free to marry and my grandmother could make things difficult for me in the meantime," said Benjie.

"How could she do that?" asked Charlie, rushing in.

"She could send me away, lock me up, or I could get hurt again like last time. I promised Miss Nancy I would marry her, and I want to be in a fit state to do it," said Benjie.

"Does she really lock people up?" asked Charlie.

"They get locked up in the outhouse right at the end of the path, and they don't get any food," said Benjie.

"That's terrible," said Charlie. "No one did that to us, even in the poorhouse; and we always got bread and water."

"There are rules about what you can do to poorhouse inmates, but some gangmasters make their own rules," said Tom. "That is why it is very important that you should keep Benjie's news to yourself. We must keep our patients' secrets; otherwise they would never trust us. You can't be a surgeon's apprentice if you gossip."

"Dr. Jarvis must know a lot of secrets," said Charlie, impressed.

"That's why my hair is white and I am old before my time!" said William, who had been standing quietly at the back.

Tom was worrying about Benjie instead of concentrating on the Harvest Festival preparations. Tom had no part in decorating the church for the special service, that was women's work, and not many of their disputes were expected to come to blows. The quoits match with the Gretna men was a different matter, and all the doctors were expected to attend in case of injury. A quoit might hit a bystander or someone could be injured during one of the heated discussions afterwards.

It was usually a good weekend for everyone to meet and exchange news and have a break from work, everyone celebrating a good harvest without a care in the world. The potatoes would not be picked until October, but all the rest of the harvest was usually gathered in before the back end of the year.

This year the work had not been finished, and Martha Armstrong's gang were two weeks behind. Some of her workers had hired themselves out directly to farmers, and Martha had unexpectedly found no replacements available from the poorhouse. The farmers were worried about getting the harvest in before the weather broke, and some of the older children were to stay home from school until the harvest was safely in.

A good result from the quoits match would cheer everyone up, but they all remembered the recent defeat at Gretna. Still, on their green with their rules, the result might be different if all the players turned up, and the new player was as good as everyone claimed.

"Are all the team ready?" asked Tom as they carried out a last inspection of the green.

"Your George is here; he will replace old Gaffer. Richard is expected to bring the new player. Jeannie's dad is poorly, so our first reserve, Adam, is playing instead. There is no sign of Ox, and usually we can rely on him," said Arthur. "None of Martha Armstrong's gang is here, they are still busy working. So we haven't got a 'shower up' to encourage the players. I suppose we could manage without one, if it came to it, but we would probably lose."

"Who did it last time?"

"Nobody when we went to Gretna, they really missed Wiggy encouraging them. "I think that is one reason they lost."

"Is there anyone else that can do it?"

"Benjie Armstrong is very good, but he is not here yet, I heard that they are all still busy. I really don't know what we shall do."

"I'll do it if you can't get anyone else, as long as no-one expects me to throw quoits. I would be patching up injuries all evening."

"That would never do," said Arthur. "My father would play if Ox isn't here. But it is nearly time to warm up and there is no sign of any of them."

"The harvest is more important; we will get some sort of a team together," said Tom, hoping he wouldn't have to play.

Players started arriving, and a crowd began to gather. Someone was running a book, with Gretna as the favourites. Kit looked very unsure of himself as he arrived with Richard for the warm up.

"What do I have to do?" asked Kit.

"It's just like last night, only different grass. The hob is like the peg we were using, and you have already practised with the quoits," said Richard.

"I'll stand near the hob again if that helps," said Charlie.

Kit made his first tentative throw.

Tom took his opportunity to put a bet on the home side, and saw that the odds had lengthened in favour of Gretna.

"You need to be a bit further to the right," said Charlie.

"There are a lot of people on that side," said Kit.

"Don't worry, they will move," said Richard.

"Are all these people watching us?" asked Kit. "Will they be cross if we lose and it is my fault?"

"Don't worry, it's not the end of the world," said Richard. "And it is always the captain's fault."

"Will I still be able to live at the forge after the game?" asked Kit.

"Yes, you are an apprentice, like Charlie is," said Richard.

Kit looked blank.

"And how else would you practice for the next match?" said Richard.

"That's much better! Near the hob! Only that much away," said Charlie, waving his hands and jumping up and down.

All the players took their turn to warm up and get used to the green, although some of them had played there many times before. Hamish had brought a full team of experienced players, and even a couple of reserves. The big Scotsmen accepted that the rules were different in England, but grumbled a bit anyway.

The game was just about to start when Ox and Frank arrived with one or two other gang members.

"We're one player short. Where's Benjie?" asked Richard.

"He has to finish his work, so he can't play," said Frank.

"Surely he could have been spared for the game!" said Arthur.

"The farmers all want their harvest in as soon as possible, and Benjie still has to move three cartloads," said Frank.

"Half the gang is still working," said Ox.

"Benjie was late home last night, that made him slow. So if you lose today, you know who to blame," said Frank.

"We can't have a team without a shower up," said Arthur.

"All he did was stand next to the hob and shout at people," said Frank. "I could do that."

"Tom said he would be a shower up if Benjie was not here in time," said Arthur.

Tom reluctantly moved forward, but Charlie was already in position.

"Charlie may as well carry on, he has been to most of the practices to help Kit and he is doing a grand job!" said Richard.

Tom was relieved that he did not have to play, and hoped that Charlie would behave himself. He was worried about Benjie, and whether he would survive until he came of age. Benjie could be broken in health and spirit, or even dead, in two years' time.

The Scots were still complaining about quoits but said that they would beat the soft Sassenachs at their own game. Frank had to be forcibly restrained, and was tactfully led inside the ale house and given a large drink.

"Since we have come all this way, we should play the best of nine," said Hamish.

"That may take a long time, with teams of seven," said Richard.

"No problem, we will beat you in five games!" shouted one of Hamish's team, who looked like a troublemaker.

"Easy!" said another Scotsman, who looked an awkward sort of lad.

Richard was trying to concentrate on the game, but kept thinking about Benjie; perhaps he would have a chance to talk to Hamish in case Nancy needed a Gretna wedding. Ox was a bit upset at the Scottish claims, but Arthur managed to smooth things over.

"If the match goes the distance the light will not be very good at the end of the evening," said Arthur. He was worried about losing profitable drinking time.

"It is bad enough playing in England with silly little quoits and different rules for each ale house," said Hamish. "If we play best of three, we will be finished in two games and it won't be worth coming."

"Perhaps it will be past bedtime for those wee English boys," said Troublemaker, singling out Charlie and Adam.

Adam turned pale, but Charlie got to his feet.

"We'll beat you if it takes all night," said Charlie.

Troublemaker and Awkward loomed over Charlie. Tom got ready to step in but Kit and Ox were there first.

"Nine games it is," said Richard, quickly.

"That should sort out the men from the boys," said Hamish.

***

It looked as if Troublemaker was right when the Gretna team easily won the first three games. Richard and Ox were playing well, but Arthur had other things on his mind, like protecting the green and looking after his customers. Adam and Kit were very nervous as this was their first match, but they were slowly improving with Charlie's encouragement and Richard's advice.

George had not played for a while, and had not been to any of the practices. Everyone knew that George was newly married, and there was speculation on why he had been away. Some of the comments from the crowd made the women blush so they moved off to set the tables for the harvest supper, as the match was nearly over.

Gretna was winning the fourth game, with only Awkward and Kit still to play. Arthur had disappeared to serve some customers, and check that the supper arrangements were all right. Some of the men were a little distracted by the food on the tables and in the confusion, Awkward fell over and his quoit was well short of the hob.

"I was tripped! I should throw that again," said Awkward.

"You fell over your own feet; they are big enough!" said Hamish.

"We'll give the Sassenachs a chance," said Troublemaker, and the rest of the team agreed with him.

Kit's quoit fell an inch from the hob, so the home team won the game unexpectedly.

"Sorry, lads, you will have to wait a few more minutes for your supper," said Hamish.

Things started looking a bit better for the home team. Kit and Adam were settling, and George was getting into his stride. Tom overheard Arthur's father telling him to concentrate on his game and let other people get on with their work. It hadn't occurred to Arthur that a close game this year would ensure more customers next year, but it was spelt out to him in no uncertain terms.

The home team narrowly won the fifth game, on merit rather than luck. Confidence grew, and it looked as if they might be playing for a bit longer. Charlie looked as sure of himself as ever, Tom wondered if he needed to be sustained. As Tom passed the supper table, he took a few small pies; after all it was in a good cause.

"Thanks, Dr. Tom, Kit and I were getting a bit peckish, and as for Adam, there is nothing of him."

"Is that enough for the three of you?"

"Could we have some of that bread and rum butter after the next couple of games? Before it all goes!"

"I will see what I can do. How much did you bet on the game?"

"I put my life savings on our team, but I am sure we will win."

It looked as if Charlie was right as the home team won the next two games but then Gretna easily won the eighth game, as some players in the home team were getting very tired. Kit was young and lacked stamina, Ox had been working hard since five in the morning, Adam looked almost dead on his feet. The Gretna men were used to throwing an eleven-pound quoit over eighteen yards, so they found it easy to throw a smaller quoit eleven yards.

The ninth game was hard fought but Adam and Kit rallied as the rum butter kicked in. Charlie got Adam to imagine that he was throwing chalk at a naughty schoolboy, and his aim improved considerably. The light was failing, so the game stretched out as players went to see where their quoits had landed. The tension was almost unbearable as there were only four throws to make. You could have heard a pin drop.

Hamish threw the best throw of the match; his quoit actually touched the hob at one side. The Gretna team did not think the throw could be improved on, until Richard's quoit touched the other side of the hob.

Troublemaker walked up to the mark, he looked as if he could have continued to play all night. The Gretna team were very proud of him and they knew they could count on him for a good throw. They were not disappointed when his quoit completely encircled the hob.

The game was as good as over and the Gretna team were gloating, when Kit stepped up to the mark. Kit was shaking a little, as he felt that everybody was watching him.

"Remember the old days, Kit, when we sat on the wall throwing stones. I said that I bet that you couldn't hit the pigeon in the next field. Best pigeon pie I ever tasted," said Charlie.

Kit remembered the pigeon, and the pie. He stopped shaking, and the quoit flew out of his hand. The light was so bad that nobody could see where it went. Kit stood, swaying on his feet, as the others went to look for the quoit. It sat on top of the hob completely covering the quoit that would have won the game for Gretna.

***

Everyone thought that it had been a very good game; although the Gretna team thought the Scottish rules would have made it more of a man's game. They also thought that the Sassenachs had been given a chance in the fourth game, and so honours were fairly even, even with English rules. Each side thought they had the better team.

The skirmishes started over the food, some of the players did not think they had their fair share, but there was plenty of food to go around, even enough to throw at each other afterwards.

Will and Tom were kept busy with cuts and bruises and the occasional dislocation. Tom's final patient was Hamish who had skinned his knuckles. On Frank, apparently.

Richard had been hoping to have a quiet word with Hamish before he went home.

"You have a good team there," said Hamish. "Promising youngsters as well."

"Don't you have younger players coming on?" asked Richard.

"They only want to play football. I don't see the point. Gretna will never be any good at football."

"I am sure the youngsters will change their minds. Are you still in the wedding business?"

"We still have our share of child brides. The extra people keep our inns and ale houses busy."

"Do the young couple always get the benefit of the doubt?"

"Mostly, otherwise they wouldn't bother. Why? Have you some customers for me?"

"Possibly. Would it matter if it was a child bridegroom?"

"That would be a novelty, but I don't see as it makes any difference."

"There's a young lad who needs to get away from his family."

"Can't you talk to the magistrates?"

"He'd prefer not to, even though he is being ill-treated," said Richard, "he hopes to bat out time for a year or so, but I thought I would ask you, just in case."

"He and his girl will be welcome at Gretna." said Hamish. "Now let's get some ale before it is all gone."

***

Tom looked for Charlie, who was sitting on the doorstep with Adam and Kit. In spite of their youth, they had been well supplied with ale and were mellow.

"Youngsters today don't know how to play quoits," said Adam.

"'S right," said Charlie.

"When I'm a teacher, I will make sure they learn," said Adam.

"Then we will be the best in England," said Charlie, thinking of his winnings.

"And still beat Gretna," said Kit.

"Every time," said Charlie.

"I feel a bit wobbly," said Adam," it must be the excitement."

Tom went back inside the ale house looking for Will, and found him with Richard and Mr. Watson, discussing how they would put the world to rights. The blacksmith and the doctor were propping up the schoolteacher, just like the three lads on the doorstep outside.

21 THE SCHOOL

The first morning of the autumn term was lovely and fresh. Nancy enjoyed her walk to school with the birdsong and wildflowers along the way. She was more aware of her surroundings than usual, and noticed the beauties of nature as never before. She hoped she wasn't turning soft.

The farmers were hoping that the weather would hold for another two weeks while they got the rest of the harvest in, with the help of one or two older children who should have been at school.

Mrs. Hull was going to be busy this morning; Nancy could hear the new children crying to go home. Soon some of the other children would join in when they realized that going home might be an option. Nancy suspected that the older children, at home with the harvest, would rather be in school.

It was the same every term, thought Nancy, as she sent two of her older girls to help Mrs. Hull. Nancy took out her ruler, and laid it purposefully on the front of her desk. Some of the newly promoted infants gasped. She took the register, looked for troublemakers and made sure they did not sit together; there were free desks at the front, just in case.

There seemed to be a lot of noise in Mr. Watson's class; it sounded as if Charlie and Adam were acting out the triumph of the local quoits team. Some of Nancy's class wanted to go and look, but changed their minds when she looked them in the eye and picked up her ruler. She wondered where Mr. Watson was, but he was on his way to her classroom.

"I need your help a bit this morning, Miss Graham. I need to show Adam the ropes, as it his first morning as a pupil teacher. Charlie Armstrong here is with us for the mornings until he catches up with his schoolwork. Can you have a little chat with Charlie and see what he needs to know?" asked Mr. Watson.

"Just let me set some work for my class first," said Nancy. This was a pointed reminder to Mr. Watson that he should make sure his pupils were occupied before he left the room. He had heard it all before and took no notice.

"Turn to Psalm 23 in your Bibles, copy the words onto your slates and learn it. I expect you to be word perfect when I get back," said Nancy. "Any noise and I will change my mind and set you Psalm 119."

Some of her older children realized that Psalm 23 was shorter, and started work quickly. The other children followed their lead, laboriously copying the words letter by letter.

It seemed to Nancy that the school could not run without her, and she had to sort everyone's problems – it made her feel very important. But what was all this about showing Adam the ropes? Nancy had to fend for herself when she started work. While she started gathering up a slate and some books, Nancy noticed that some of the older boys were giggling at Charlie who was making faces behind Mr. Watson's back. Nancy's hand itched for her cane, but Charlie looked so much like his cousin Benjie she decided to ignore the misbehaviour for now. Maybe she *was* turning soft.

"My class will do their work in silence," said Nancy, and she left the classroom door open as she assessed Charlie's standard of work.

Charlie seemed to enjoy reading, and had reached a good standard by reading whatever he could find in the surgery. Nancy thought that most of the doctor's books were unsuitable for someone of Charlie's tender age, and made a mental note to mention it to Tom later. Nancy set Charlie some addition to do; he failed to keep the numbers in the right columns and the result was a mess. Charlie's handwriting was appalling and he spelt words exactly as he spoke them.

"It looks as if you have a bit of catching up to do," said Nancy. "Off you go to Mr. Watson for the time being, and the teachers will discuss which class is best for you. Handwriting is very important; people need to read what doctors have written."

"Dr. Tom's writing is terrible and nobody can read it," said Charlie." I thought it was supposed to be like that."

Nancy was not sure whether Charlie was being impertinent, but he looked very innocent. She tried to keep a straight face, but decided that he needed a word or two of advice from her.

"Charlie, you are here to learn as much as you can, and your behaviour must be perfect. The boys will look to you as a leader, and you mustn't lead them astray or nobody will learn anything. You have been given a great opportunity to be a surgeon's apprentice, I don't want to have to tell Dr.

Tom that you are too troublesome to teach."

"Yes, miss," said Charlie, as he decided to keep his frog in his pocket and not introduce it into the classroom.

Nancy went back to her class, asked the children to own up if they had been talking while she was away, and three hands reluctantly went up. The three miscreants lined up in a sorry little row, with their hands outstretched. Nancy picked up her ruler from the desk and flexed it. Perhaps she wasn't getting soft after all.

***

Later, when the children had gone home to lunch, the teachers discussed the arrangements for the term.

"It looks as if Charlie needs more writing practice. I can arrange that quite easily," said Mr. Watson.

"Everyone wanted to sit next to him and he chose Susan," said Adam.

"It'll probably do him good to copy a bit from her," said Mr. Watson." All the new children in my class are very good workers."

Nancy wished she could say the same for her new pupils from Mrs. Hull's class. What had the woman been teaching them for the past two years?

"There is nothing wrong with Charlie's mental arithmetic," said Adam. "He wouldn't let himself be short-changed when he collected the winnings from his bet."

"That's as maybe but I think I need to set Charlie some written work to make sure that he has grasped the principles. Bets are all very well, but they are not real arithmetic," said Nancy. The two men looked at her; they knew better but decided not to argue.

 "Charlie shall do the same work as my class," said Mr. Watson. "He should have caught up by Christmas, possibly earlier. You have enough to do with your class of forty-five."

Nancy was about to give a piece of her mind on class management when another voice spoke unexpectedly.

"Let the men decide, dear," said Mrs. Hull. "They know best; they have more experience of the world than we have."

Nancy was speechless; she didn't see that at all. All Adam knew was what the teachers had taught him. Mr. Watson might have known a lot at one time, but he had forgotten it all now. "We will continue with three classes for the time being, since one member of staff feels so strongly about it," said Mr. Watson.

"Adam can tidy your cupboards and fill the inkwells. Maybe do some marking and hear some of the children read," said Nancy.

"I need someone to hear my older children read while I try and settle the new ones. I will be glad when we have four smaller classes," said Mrs. Hull.

"I can manage quite well, thank you," said Nancy.

"Adam can teach my class in the afternoons while I catch up with my paperwork," said Mr. Watson. "Later on, I will show him what paperwork needs to be done."

"He will be headmaster here one day, so he needs to know," said Mrs. Hull. "The board would never appoint a woman as a head teacher."

So Nancy knew what she had always suspected, that she would never live in the schoolhouse and run the school. Instead it would be some incompetent man, and she would have to pick up the pieces without the authority, the recognition and the better pay. She wished Elizabeth could have started as a pupil teacher instead of Adam, but Nancy had been overruled because of Elizabeth's attendance record. But Nancy now knew that the board would have brought in a new male head teacher anyway.

***

Nancy was still thinking about the school when she waited for Benjie, three days later. Nancy decided not to worry about being head teacher, and the schoolhouse that went with it. She would be a married woman in two years' time, and she would not be allowed to teach. Mrs. Hull was allowed to teach, but she was a widow and had previously run a 'dame' school in her kitchen. Most married women had enough to do without going out to work; they looked after a man, children and the house. But some women took in washing or sewing, and many of the poorer women had to work in the mill. Nancy realized that she looked after her father, her sisters and the house as well as teaching at the school. Would a married woman's role be enough to keep her busy?

Nancy felt that if she didn't interfere in the school, things would not be done properly. She didn't want her new cousin Charlie to be at a disadvantage because of Mr. Watson's laziness. Perhaps she would have a word with Benjie when he came to see her.

But Benjie didn't arrive on the day she expected him. That night Nancy felt devastated because she was sure that Benjie didn't want to see her anymore. Then she lay awake, panicking, wondering what could have happened to him.

***

In the morning, with the sun shining, the world looked very different, and she was sure that the gang had been working until dark and Benjie had not been able to get away.

On Friday afternoons Adam was to take the top class for cricket, and only the naughty children would be left in the class doing extra work. Nancy's class looked at her hopefully; they felt that they had worked very hard and deserved a treat, and she felt under pressure to provide one. Perhaps she could take them for a walk, give them a little fresh air before winter set in. They could improve their minds by learning about the plants and animals on their way.

Nancy lined her children up in a little crocodile, two by two, and thought about the route that they would take for their walk; previous experience had taught her not to go too near the river. Nancy thought that it was too early to go anywhere near the horse chestnut trees; in a week or two the children would be able to gather all their conkers from the ground. Now there would be no fallen conkers, and the boys would want to climb the trees to find them. In the past she found it very tedious coaxing children down from the trees.

"Can we go that way, miss, near the wild raspberries?"

"Please, miss!"

Nancy gave in to the little chorus of requests, and they set off towards the fields where Ma Armstrong's gang was working. She saw Benjie, in the distance, tending to the horse. Nancy was glad to see that he was all right, and stopped for a minute for the younger children to catch up. Benjie saw her, lifted his cap, and the sun came out from behind a cloud.

***

A few days later, Nancy was waiting at home in case Benjie called, but it was already late in the evening. Sally and Susan had already gone to bed when there was a knock on the back door.

"Benjie, it's so good to see you," said Nancy, running into his arms.

"Careful Miss Nancy, I am very dirty, I came straight from the fields. I must go back before I am missed, but I just had to see you. To see if it was all real and you cared for me. It all seems such a long way from my life at home," said Benjie.

"I love you Benjie, and I count the hours until I see you again," said Nancy, wondering if she had time to lead him astray again.

"I really love you, Miss Nancy," said Benjie, resisting the pull in the direction of the hayloft. "I think we need to be really careful because of your reputation; we could stay in this room and talk for a bit." But he didn't let go of her hand.

Nancy would have preferred a roll in the hay, but didn't argue. She knew Benjie had her interests at heart, but it felt really strange to do as she was told. She knew that Benjie had more experience of the world than she had, unlike the men she worked with. Richard stomped in from the forge, very loudly, and Nancy realized that she had forgotten about him.

"I want to thank you for what you are doing for Charlie," said Benjie. "He showed me his writing, and it is much easier to read."

"I wanted to set him his own work, but Mr. Watson insisted on treating him like the rest of his class. I think he is learning more from Susan than Mr. Watson," said Nancy.

"And who taught Susan?" said Richard. "She is a credit to you, and to all of us."

"I feel that I am fighting a losing battle in the school. The children know nothing when they come into my class from Mrs. Hull. Mr. Watson isn't as firm with them as he should be, and they do not always learn from him," said Nancy.

"You're quite right to make sure that they learn as much as possible in your class," said Richard. "If our local children learn to read and write properly, they have more choice in what they do. They have a chance to work in an office or a shop; in the old days the choice was between the fields and the mill, and the best jobs would go to incomers. You, Jeannie and Tom would not have had a chance to better yourselves without learning to read and write. It is good for the town if we have a school where the children learn."

"The board understands that. Mrs. Hull is really minding the little ones so that their mothers can work, so anything the infant class learn from her is a bonus," continued Richard, "Mr. Watson was born into a gentleman's family, where book learning was taken for granted, so he doesn't see things quite as we do. Adam will see things your way, once he has found his feet. He comes from an ordinary family and is grateful for the chance that you and the school have given him."

"But they are giving the children a reward for good behaviour," said Nancy." The children play silly games on Friday afternoons instead of digging the garden or doing sewing."

"It won't do the children any harm to have a bit of fresh air once a week," said Richard. "Childhood is very short."

"It was lovely to see you out with the children," said Benjie "It fair made my day."

"They looked a bit sorry for themselves so I took them out for a nature walk. They learnt from it, it wasn't just playing," said Nancy.

"They learn from the games too," said Richard. "Taking turns, watching what they are doing, working as a team. I am hoping that Adam will find me some quoits players; it will be good for Gorton. We were a bit lucky in the Gretna match."

Nancy hadn't thought about things like that; maybe her father had a wider view than she had.

"Sometimes I won't be able to come and see you, so it is lovely to catch a glimpse of you on Fridays," said Benjie.

Nancy thought that it wouldn't do any harm to have one or two more nature walks, and she could choose the route carefully. Once the brambles had all gone, and the weather was colder, she would make sure that the children settled down to something more useful.

22 THE QUARRYMAN

Benjie went home that night with lightness in his step because he had persuaded Nancy that they needed to take care and preserve her reputation. He felt that too many visits to the hayloft might result in a love child and a very public visit to the magistrate to ask for the wedding to be brought forward.

He couldn't get away to visit her for the following three weeks so it was wonderful to see Nancy and her class on Fridays; their nature walks took them past where he was working. Nancy looked like a real lady and he thought that she was much too good for the likes of him. Benjie could hardly believe that she loved him, and never forgot how lucky he was.

It took Benjie a while to get ready to go and see Nancy, as he was covered in mud after the potato picking; after a cold wash in the yard, he set off in his Sunday best.

***

Martha Armstrong and Frank were waiting for Benjie when he got back from visiting Nancy.

"Where do you think you have been?" asked Martha.

"Just out," said Benjie.

"Have you been to see that cousin of yours, with his posh job at the doctor's?" asked Martha.

"I might have been," said Benjie.

"Your friend the doctor has been interfering again. I don't know what he has been saying at the poorhouse. We wanted another labourer to replace Wiggy, but the Master said he didn't have any," said Martha.

"There were only two young lads the right age this year, and they both got work somewhere else," said Benjie.

"Younger lads would have done, but the Master chose to keep them idling away in the poorhouse for another year. He said they were not ready to be working long hours in all weathers; I don't know where he got that idea. Your doctor friend must be lying about us, he can be very sneaky," said Martha.

"Old men would have done," said Frank.

"Perhaps they refused," said Benjie. That was not a good move, and the blow to the side of his head sent him staggering.

"I don't think you have been to see your friend. I think you have been out courting. Look at him in his Sunday suit!" said Martha.

"Which trollop would want Benjie?" asked Frank.

Benjie managed to land a blow before he hit the floor.

When Benjie woke up he found he had been locked in the outhouse again. He didn't mind too much, as it gave him a rest, especially from all the questions that he would not want to answer. He was more worried about his Sunday best clothes; they were torn in places. Benjie resolved to get his suit to Charlie for safe keeping as soon as he had the chance, as Charlie would know where to get it mended. Benjie heard the key turn in the lock.

"You've one more day potato picking, and you will start work in the quarry first thing the day after," said Martha. "That will put a stop to your courting."

"Will I be living in their barracks?" asked Benjie.

"I'm not paying good money for you, Ox and young Caleb to live a life of luxury in the barracks," said Martha. "You will walk from here every morning; I expect you will be skiving off with the packhorses most days."

Benjie knew better than to argue, and slowly got to his feet.

"Get a move on, those potatoes must be harvested today. Everyone else is ready to go, and you have missed breakfast," said Martha.

Benjie would have preferred to spend the winter hedge laying and ditch digging, so that he could work shorter hours. This would give him time to see Charlie and spend a lot of time with Nancy. The long walk to the quarry in the mornings, and back in the evenings, would leave him with no free time.

The work might be all right, taking the packhorses to the coast so that the slate could be loaded on to the ships. If only he could get a message to Nancy to say that he would not be able to see her for a while. Perhaps she would think that he didn't love her anymore; he couldn't bear the thought of that.

***

The work in the quarry was much worse than Benjie expected. The skilled quarrymen blasted the slate out of the ground with gunpowder, and then the large pieces were bored and blasted again. The men used sledgehammers and wedges to make the pieces small enough to carry to the riving shed. The skilled rivers split the stone into thin sheets, and the dresser shaped them into slates with a special heavy knife.

Benjie was hired as a labourer; it was his job to move the slate from one part of the site to another, dodging the blasting and falling stones. It was very dangerous work and there were many injuries among the men; there had been one or two deaths in the past. As the days got shorter, and the light got worse, it was even more difficult to see what he was doing, and he was lucky to get away with just cuts and bruises.

Once in a while Benjie got the chance to take a cartload of slate to the town, which made a nice change from all the noise in the quarry. Once he took the packhorses to the coast; that was grand, walking across the fells. Apart from that he enjoyed the walk to work in the mornings, the three of them quiet in the early morning silence. The walk back in the evening was not quite as good as they all had the aches, pains and grumbles from their day's work.

Benjie was looking forward to Christmas; his day holiday would be very welcome as he could see Nancy again and this thought was keeping him going as he worked on the slate in mid-December. The light was going fast; Benjie and Ox were working on the slate with sledgehammers, trying not to injure themselves in the process.

Young Caleb was carrying slate to the riving sheds, dodging the falling stone, when he slipped on some loose stone and slid down to the bottom of the quarry. When Caleb didn't get up again, Benjie went over to see what was wrong; the lad had fallen awkwardly, with his leg bent under him. When Benjie tried to straighten his leg, the shinbone was visible through his skin.

The foreman came over; Benjie was glad because he did not know what to do

"I saw one of the doctors pass on the road below, must have been on his way to a farm. One of the men has gone to fetch him; he can set Caleb's leg for him. Otherwise Caleb would never be able to walk again," said the foreman.

"Has this happened before?" asked Benjie.

"Quite often, if a man has had his leg set, he sits in the barracks, dressing slate, until he can walk again. If we carry Caleb out of the way of the blasting, you can sit with him until the doctor comes," said the foreman.

There was no way to make Caleb comfortable while he was being carried, but there was no alternative. Benjie felt that he was waiting with Caleb for hours, worrying whether he would ever get better. He didn't know what was worse, his cries when he was awake, or the death like faint he kept slipping into. Caleb was only fifteen, and had a widowed mother living in the town.

Benjie was pleased to see the doctor; he felt that Dr. Tom could make anyone better. Tom looked at Caleb's leg and was not so sure, if they had been at the infirmary or the surgery it would have been a lot easier. The bleeding had stopped, but the lad had lost quite a lot of blood. Tom gave Caleb a drop of brandy so that he would not feel his leg being set and splinted, but he threw it up straight away.

Tom reduced the fracture as best he could, but could not set it as well as he would have done in the surgery. He splinted the limb, and they were all set on carrying Caleb to the barracks, when the lad insisted that he wanted to go home to his mother. The foreman said that the slate cart was ready to go to the town, and Caleb could travel on that if he wanted.

Tom hesitated; he did not think the journey would do Caleb any good at all. On the other hand, perhaps he could set the leg better at the surgery so that Caleb would have less of a limp when he got better. Caleb was determined to go home, so they got the cart ready.

"Will he be all right?" asked Benjie.

"I hope so," said Tom, out of earshot of Caleb. "His mother will help him pull through, if it is meant to be. It is a very nasty break. Are there a lot of accidents here?"

"Quite a few, the skilled quarrymen are usually all right; the rest of us are bad at keeping out of the way of the falling stones. We are not so good at staying out of the way of the blasting. Caleb was running when he slipped; it is very difficult to run on this scree," said Benjie.

Tom watched the men working as the cart was prepared for Caleb; he could not see how it was possible for the labourers to do their job safely.

"Have you any messages for Charlie or Nancy?" asked Tom.

"Just tell them that I am working here long hours, but I hope to see them at Christmas," said Benjie.

Tom arranged Caleb on the cart, and Benjie said goodbye to him, knowing that his friend would be in safe hands. With a shiver, he wondered what would have happened if Tom had not been visiting one of the nearby farms.

23 THE ACCIDENT

Caleb slept for the first half of the journey; Tom was quite optimistic as he rode alongside the cart but the second half of the journey was more harrowing. Caleb must have felt every jolt on the rough road and Tom would never forget his screams. The worst part of the journey was Caleb's arrival home, and the look on his mother's face when she saw her son lying in the cart, unable to move.

The first week went well, then the exhaustion, the cold, the shock was all too much for a boy of fifteen. In spite of Tom's best efforts, Caleb had caught a chill and was sinking fast.

On Christmas Eve Tom got the call he didn't want.

***

Tom sank down into a chair when he came home from Caleb's house, and hid his head in his hands.

"There's nothing more you could have done," said William.

"The injury was healing, I was sure he would be all right," said Tom.

"He had a five mile walk to the quarry, a day of back breaking work, and the walk home. He has done that every day since October. He had no strength left," said William.

"He was so young."

"Caleb was not the first, and he won't be the last. That is what makes this job so hard. I can help you with the report for the Coroner; make sure that we do not miss any contributory factors."

"Could the same kind of accident happen to Benjie?"

"Benjie will be lucky to survive until he is of age."

"What will happen to Caleb's mother now?" asked Tom, as the stark fact of Benjie's future slowly sank in.

"She takes in washing, but the money from Caleb helped to pay the rent so she will find it hard."

"Has she any other family?"

"None living. She will probably end up in the poorhouse. I suppose there are worse places to be."

"I need to tell Benjie about Caleb's death." said Tom. "Has he been in yet?"

"He called in to see Charlie, brought some clothes that needed mending. Charlie was all for taking them to Jeannie, but I made him take a look first. Can't let all that tailoring training go to waste," said William.

Charlie heard his name and came into the shop, glad of a break from sewing.

"Benjie came in to see us, and went on to Nancy's. Shall I fetch him?" asked Charlie hopefully.

"No, I'll go, you are busy," said Tom.

***

When Tom knocked on the door at the blacksmith's and Susan let him in, Richard, Benjie and Nancy were sitting near the fire, eating the toast that Sally was making for them. The tea things were on the table. Tom did not want to disturb the happy gathering, and felt like going back.

"How is Caleb?" asked Benjie, but one look at Tom's face told him everything.

"We lost him," said Tom bleakly. He sat down but waved away the proffered toast.

"I am sure you did all you could," said Benjie, sadly. "I will miss him very much. Is his mother all right?"

"I don't know," said Tom. "I hope so." Sally gave him a cup of tea, which he needed.

"Are there many accidents at the quarry?" asked Richard.

"Too many, especially among the labourers; you could be next, Benjie," said Tom.

"What shall we do?" wailed Nancy. Sally thought the obvious answer was more tea, and set about providing it.

"I'll be all right," said Benjie, who was still thinking about Caleb.

"I think you should bring the wedding forward," said Richard, and there was a gasp from Nancy.

"I'll be fine," said Benjie. He must not let Nancy's family undermine his pride.

"We could go to the magistrates, "said Richard.

"Never!" said Benjie.

"But it will take too long, and they might not give permission unless I say…" said Nancy.

"Say what?" asked Susan, innocently.

"Never you mind," said Richard.

"If we, sort of, explained matters to the magistrates," said Nancy.

"Over my dead body," said Benjie.

"It probably will be," said Tom.

"Gretna Green it is, then," said Richard.

"I would rather wait until I am of age, and get married like a man," said Benjie.

"You might not have the choice," said Tom.

"But I don't want to be carried off like a child bride," said Benjie.

"How can you let your silly male pride get in the way of our happiness," said Nancy and burst into tears, waving away the cup of tea.

"Now look what you have done," said Susan. "You will get yourself killed, and Nancy will die of a broken heart."

"Or turn into a cross old maid," said Sally, who felt that the process was already starting.

"I will do what Nancy thinks best," said Benjie, giving in. Tom thought that Benjie had a lot to learn.

"When will you go?" asked Susan.

"Now would be best," said Tom, remembering William's forebodings.

"I need my best clothes; I can't get married like this," said Benjie. "I don't know how long Jeannie will take to do the mending."

"There wasn't much damage and Charlie has started on the work," said Tom. "He should be nearly finished by now."

"We will go and help Nancy with her packing," said Susan, hoping she would leave behind one or two things she didn't want.

"I will get the dowry ready," said Richard.

"I don't feel good about a dowry, you have been so kind, I don't want to take anything from you. And people will think I am a fortune hunter," said Benjie.

Nancy burst into tears again and Tom idly wondered if it would have made any difference to him if he had known that Nancy had a dowry. He decided that it probably wouldn't have done.

"All my girls will have a dowry, I won't live forever and there are no pockets in shrouds," said Richard.

Sally and Susan started getting upset as they hoped that their father would live forever. Nancy wondered who would get the forge.

"But I can never pay you back," said Benjie.

"Keep it in the family, pass something on to your own daughters," said Richard. Nancy blushed, Sally and Susan giggled.

"I can't go now, not before Caleb's funeral," said Benjie.

"The funeral will be next week, after the inquest," said Tom.

Benjie's next holiday was New Year's Day, and they decided that there would be an excellent opportunity to leave for Gretna while the men from Martha's gang were at the ale house the night before. What could possibly go wrong? Tom left them discussing details and went back to the surgery to make his report.

***

Tom knew that his mother was expecting him home for the rest of Christmas Eve, and for Christmas day. Tom was really looking forward to spending time with his family as his mother's cooking would be much better than Charlie's. He would go home as soon as he had written his accident report for the Coroner; it would not take long.

"Mother sent me to fetch you, we haven't seen you for ages. I thought you were going to get away early for Christmas," said Mary Ann, who came into the shop.

"I just had a bit of work to finish, it took longer than I expected," said Tom. "A few more minutes will do it."

"I thought Dr. Jarvis was on duty at Christmas this year," said Mary Ann. She was wandering around the shop, looking at things, picking them up and putting them down. Tom wondered what she would make of the jar of leeches.

"Nearly finished. I have responsibilities, you know," said Tom trying to sound grown up.

"We are having goose for Christmas dinner this year, it is really big. We stuffed a pillow with all the feathers," said Mary Ann.

"I can't wait," said Tom, thinking of all the Christmas food. "There, that is done, I am all set."

"I was wondering about something."

"And?"

"Can I ask you something? "You won't mind?"

"No, I won't mind," said Tom, wondering what was bothering her.

"You aren't courting Nancy, are you? Only you said at George's wedding that you weren't."

"Why do you think I might be courting Nancy?" Tom picked his words with care.

"Talk is that Nancy is courting, but Sally and Susan won't talk about it, and I wondered if it was you."

"Why do people think that Nancy is courting?"

"She is much nicer than she used to be. Doesn't use the cane as much. And she even took the children for walks in the nice weather. We never went for walks when I was in her class." Obviously Mary Ann had a grudge.

"I think there is too much talk about other people's business."

"I just wondered if it was you, I don't suppose I would really mind."

"It isn't me, but please can I ask you not to talk about it; there is a very

111

good reason. If you hear any more, can you please tell me? I will let you know what is happening as soon as I can, but it is not my secret to tell." Tom looked worried.

"Sorry, I didn't mean to listen to gossip, I don't usually. Is there anything I can do to help?"

"It would help if you just didn't talk about Nancy for a bit. Is there any other interesting gossip about?"

"Yes, Adam keeps asking how Elizabeth is. "I wonder if…""

"Urgent letter for you again, Tom," said Arthur, who had just rushed into the shop.

Tom opened the letter:

Dear Tom
We need your help. Come quickly or it will be too late.
Your brother
Joe

"Can you ask your stable lads to get Thunderbolt ready for me?" asked Tom.

"Right away!" said Arthur. "Are you going far?"

"I have been called out to a patient," said Tom.

"What shall I tell mother?" asked Mary Ann when Arthur had gone.

"Joe wants me to go to him urgently, but I am not sure why and I don't want her worrying until I know what is wrong," said Tom, hoping that Elizabeth was well. "It would really help if you could tell her I have been called out to a patient."

Mary Ann was thrilled that she had been told something that had to be kept secret from her mother.

"It is a good idea not to tell Arthur, he is such a gossip," she said.

24 THE FELLS

Tom hadn't realized how far he had to travel to get to Hilltop; he was very weary by the time he arrived, and so was Thunderbolt. Tom would have spared his horse the long journey, but it was too late on Christmas Eve for a mail coach. And it all sounded so urgent; he hoped he wasn't too late.

Joe came running out to meet him, giving orders to the ostlers about looking after the horse.

"That horse of yours is no thunderbolt, it took you ages to get here," said Joe.

"We did our best, he is a very fast horse, but it was a long way," said Tom. "Am I in time?"

"You are too late, Alice and her new daughter did not wait for you, they managed fine with the help of the midwife."

"Is Elizabeth all right?"

"Of course she is, why wouldn't she be?"

"Is she coughing?"

"She had a bit of a cough when she first came, but she is fine now. Come and see everybody, now you are here," said Joe.

Tom struggled down from the horse; he was cold and he ached everywhere. He walked stiffly inside.

"Come and sit down by the fire."

"I would rather stand, thank you."

"I'm sorry," said Joe. "I didn't think, I would have sent a carter for you but we hadn't one free, we never have. I would have spared you that ride if I could."

"I am fine," said Tom, "just a little stiff after the ride."

Elizabeth had put on weight and looked really well.

"Isn't your new niece beautiful, just like her mother," said Elizabeth.

Tom had seen a lot of new born babies, but was always polite enough to admire them.

***

Tom spent Christmas Day and Boxing Day with his brother's family, and prepared to go home the next day when he had recovered from the long ride. The baby was thriving, so Tom had no excuse for staying any longer. He had to get home for the inquest, so he knew he would have to force himself back onto Thunderbolt. The ride back should be easier; he told himself, there was no hurry, and it would be downhill.

"When can I go home?" asked Elizabeth, when they were all sitting near the fire.

"If you go home too soon, and work in the mill, you might be poorly again," said Tom.

"We need your help here, until Alice is back on her feet," said Joe.

"And did Adam play in the quoits match? Did he help them win?" asked Elizabeth.

Tom told the story of the quoits match, with the emphasis on George's part in the game.

"I would love to go home soon; if I promise not to work in the mill for a while, can I go?" said Elizabeth.

"You can't go just yet, there is no transport. It is really difficult to get carters to stay here, so they are run off their feet. That is why we don't visit as much as we would like. You wouldn't want to go back with Tom on Thunderbolt, would you?" said Joe.

"Believe me, you wouldn't," said Tom. "Do you need another carter here at Hilltop, Joe?"

"Do you know of one?" asked Joe. "That would be grand."

"I have a friend who is setting up as a carter," said Tom. "But he would be looking for somewhere to stay for a while."

"He would be more than welcome to stay here," said Joe.

Elizabeth looked forward to going home, but wondered who was moving to Hilltop, and why Mary Ann hadn't mentioned it.

***

When Tom made his weary way back to the surgery, Mary Ann was waiting for him in the shop.

"Are they all right?"

"All fine. Alice has a baby daughter. Elizabeth is much better, and may be coming home soon."

"That will please mother. She was a bit cross about you missing Christmas dinner."

"It couldn't be helped." said Tom. Elizabeth cooked a good dinner at Joe's, but he regretted missing the goose at home. "What is the news here?"

"Well," said Mary Ann, starting on her favourite subject, "You will never guess what they are saying about Nancy!"

"Go on."

"They say she is going to run away to get married."

"Why do they say that?"

"Mr. Graham won't do any work for anyone until he has fixed his cart. Jeannie won't do any sewing for anybody until she has made some things for Nancy, and it looks like a trousseau! And they thought she was courting anyway."

"Who do they think she is running away with?"

"They are not sure, there are all sorts of rumours. They know it isn't you because you are both of full age. And Mr. Graham must agree with it if he is fixing his cart. I didn't say anything, like you said."

"Thank you, that will really help her."

"I am not sure that I want to help her," said Mary Ann. "She is a bit quick getting out her ruler. None of the other teachers are like that."

"It'll help me. If she marries, then mother won't keep asking me when I am going to settle down," said Tom.

"I hadn't thought, I suppose she wouldn't teach at the school any more if she gets married," said Mary Ann hopefully.

"It would help if people were thrown off the scent a bit."

"How?"

"If they thought she was running away with me. Perhaps I will ask Jeannie to make me a couple of shirts urgently."

"But why would you run away to get married?"

"I didn't want a big fuss. I didn't want to spend my wedding night patching people up after a big party and all the fighting. Or Nancy wanted a romantic runaway marriage. I am sure you will think of something."

"Are you asking your little sister to tell lies?"

"Not if you don't want to. I know it is wrong."

"Yes," said Mary Ann, "but I'll enjoy it. Do you promise that it isn't you?"

"I promise," said Tom. "I suppose we had better go and see mother now. She will be pleased about Joe and Alice. They are going to call their baby Sarah."

***

Two days later, the Coroner was questioning Tom at the inquest. William was there for moral support, but Tom found the questioning mild compared to the questions from his mother two days earlier.

"What were the contributing factors to the death," asked the Coroner.

"The injury, the loss of blood, the long journey home, exhaustion and the fever," said Tom.

"Always difficult to avoid fevers," said the Coroner. "When did you start treating him for it?"

"I went to him as soon as I was called," said Tom. A murmur of agreement went around the court. "But he was too weak to fight the illness."

"Who decided to take him home?"

"He insisted on going home to his mother. We couldn't talk him out of it. It certainly didn't help, but he might have died anyway and it is always better to die at home."

"Could the accident have been avoided?" asked the Coroner, addressing the quarry foreman.

"Caleb slipped because he was running; the labourers are not always sure footed," said the foreman.

"Why was he running?"

"To get out of the way of the blasting,"

"Was there no warning?"

"You can't always tell which direction, or how bad the blast is going to be. Even with experience."

"Is there no way everyone can keep out of the quarry during blasting?"

"It would slow down the work too much, we would not make our orders, and we would all be out of work. It's possible to dodge the blasting."

"Most of the accidents happen to labourers, rather than your skilled men. Can you see any reason why?"

"The skilled men have been working on the site for a while, the labourers come from gangs that usually do farm work and they have a lot to learn. It is very hard work; the men in the prime of life are usually all right, but the gangmasters mostly send boys and old men. A young lad can get tired and careless, and make mistakes. Our men all live in the barracks at the site, but many of the labourers live at home and walk to work so that the gangmasters can save money. This lad walked five miles to work and back every day," said the foreman.

"I'm going to recommend that you employ men and encourage them to live in the barracks wherever possible," said the Coroner. "And make sure that they learn about the blasting before they start."

"Are you the gangmaster in question, Mrs. Armstrong?" he asked.

"Yes sir. I am only an old woman, and if my lads didn't get work we would all starve," said Martha.

"Is there any reason why you sent a young boy to work in the quarry? And expected him to walk such a long distance each day?"

"I didn't know the work was so dangerous! I sent my own little grandson to work at the quarry! I hope he will be all right and that he will be looked after properly," said Martha, dabbing her eyes with her handkerchief.

"And does your little grandson walk to work each day or does he stay in the barracks during the week?"

"We can't afford their prices, times are hard," whined Martha.

"I recommend that you send no more under age boys, or old men to the quarry. I also recommend that if any of your men are working in the quarry, they stay in the barracks," said the Coroner.

"I will try," said Martha.

"I don't want to see you here again under similar circumstances," said the Coroner. "Is that understood? It could be your grandson next time."

"You really know how to upset an old woman," snivelled Martha, applying the handkerchief again.

"The verdict is misadventure," said the Coroner.

Tom thought that the result was as good as could be hoped for. With Martha and the foreman accusing each other of negligence, it was impossible to say where the blame should lie. Tom had been instrumental in pointing out a problem, but he did not think the parties would leave on good terms.

25 THE CLIFFHANGER

When the foreman went back to the quarry, he made sure that Ox and Benjie got a little more time to rest during the day. Unfortunately, Martha refused to let them stay at the barracks so they still had a long walk twice a day, a sad walk without Caleb.

Benjie didn't know what the doctor was making a fuss about; he was sure he could carry out the quarry work very well without danger to himself or others. He would have preferred to work his time at the quarry, and get married as a man at twenty-one.

However, he had promised to run off with Nancy next week, and he couldn't go back on that. But where would they go? What would they live on? How would they manage? Nancy, such a lovely girl! How could she possibly care for the likes of him, a country lad with no prospects? If he worked for her father, it would hurt his pride; people would say that Benjie was no good if he needed his wife's family to help him. He would be a kept man! Benjie could imagine the taunts.

But Nancy was getting all upset on his account, worried about his safety at the quarry. Benjie wished he could show her how well he could cope. He ran along to pick up the next load, as he was getting a bit behind. He took care to go along the top of the quarry, as there was blasting further down. He could hear the noise underneath; it seemed to be getting louder, but he was safe enough on the grass at the top. Benjie ran along, thinking more of Nancy than where he was putting his feet.

The blasting was getting louder, the weather worse, and the whole of the edge of the quarry gave way. As the ground disappeared from under his feet, Benjie knew that he would be killed outright if he fell all the way to the bottom of the quarry. A tree root broke his fall, and he grabbed at it in a panic. He could see the edge of the ground a few feet above him, but could not scramble out of danger because there was no firm handhold or foothold.

Benjie knew he was going to die as soon as he let go of the tree. He managed to lever himself up a little way, but still could not reach safety. His tired arms were giving way, but he braced himself against the tree, which creaked a little.

Benjie thought of Nancy; he had been so close to happiness. If only he had let himself be talked into the trip to Gretna on Christmas Eve. Everyone else thought it would be more sensible to go straight away; it was only his pride that let them down. And it was all a waste of time, because neither he nor Ox had been allowed to go to Caleb's funeral. The foreman was willing to let them go, but they would have lost half a day's pay and Martha had flatly refused.

Benjie shouted for help, but he knew that there was nobody near enough, and his shouts would go unheard. Nobody would hear him because of the wind and the blasting. Benjie found a handhold just above him to the right, and stretched to try and grab it. He levered himself up a little and put one foot on the tree root, this move relieved his arms a little.

The sound of the blasting seemed to fade into the distance, and Benjie wondered if he was losing consciousness. If he let go, all his troubles would be over, no more criticism, taunts, bullying or beatings. His grandmother and Frank would not trouble him anymore if he just closed his eyes and let go. But then he would never marry Nancy.

Benjie could feel the rain turn to sleet, and every muscle in his body was hurting. He could smell the grass above him; perhaps he was nearer the top than he thought. He managed to move his lower foot up to the tree, which was creaking more loudly. Benjie thought the tree might not hold him for much longer and the blasting seemed to have stopped, so he shouted again.

Benjie stretched to the edge of the turf on his left; he took a good handful of grass and hoped that it would stay firm. He wedged his left foot in a previous handhold and eased himself up a little. The tree started slipping, so he had to find another foothold quickly. His final push against the tree dislodged it completely; he felt sick as he heard it crash to the bottom of the quarry. He was now far enough over the edge to grab another handful of grass.

He was halfway over the edge; so near and yet so far. Benjie's hands were slipping, his arms in agony, it would be so easy just to let go. He could see someone coming; if only he could hold firm. He thought of Nancy and gritted his teeth and held on long enough for Ox and the foreman to pull him to safety.

***

Benjie thought of his narrow escape, as he and Ox walked home in silence. The weather was appalling, but they were both looking forward to the New Year's Eve celebrations for different reasons. The ale house put on a really good spread to go with the New Year ale, and Ox had been thinking about it all day. He hoped he would have time to enjoy it before the food fight started, so he quickened his pace. Benjie was thinking about his escape; it was planned that he would wait until the rest of the gang was in the ale house before he made his move.

Benjie was going to call in at the surgery before he met Nancy; there would be plenty of time to pick up his Sunday best clothes and get changed. Charlie was looking after some money for him, tips saved when he was working in the stables. There wasn't much, and there might be even less because he had given Charlie permission to put one or two bets on for him. He rather regretted that now.

It was dark when they finally got to Martha's cottage, where the rest of the gang was getting ready for the evening celebrations. He was pleased to see them, but not so pleased to see Ma and Frank.

"You must have been telling lies about us again," said Martha.

"Me, never!" said Benjie.

"Your doctor friend has been telling lies at the inquest, he must have got them from you. Saying that the quarry work was too hard for Caleb! A bit of hard work never hurt anybody," said Martha.

Benjie bit back the retort; this was not a good time to argue.

"And your friend the foreman was saying that we should only send big strong men to the quarry. What would happen to the rest of you if we did that!" said Martha.

"That's right," said Frank.

"Taking the bread out of our mouths," said Martha. "We would all starve if you youngsters were not allowed to work."

Benjie looked for Ox to back him up, but he was nowhere to be seen.

"I'll have to teach you a lesson, again, if you can't keep quiet. No New Year for you. Lock him up, Frank!" ordered Martha.

"With pleasure," said Frank.

The outhouse had no terrors for Benjie; he was very familiar with it, as were the rest of the gang. Someone would realize he was missing, get the key from the usual place and let him out.

But Frank was more rough than usual as he forced Benjie into the outhouse, and he put the key in his pocket.

26 THE DOWRY

Nancy was preparing for her journey, and her sisters were very keen to help her. Susan was inheriting Nancy's small attic bedroom, and Sally was to take over the bedroom and bed the twins had previously shared.

"You must get all your things out of my bedroom, Susan," said Sally. "I can't possibly tidy it when it is full of your stuff."

"I need to clear more space first," said Susan, "your room is bigger than mine."

"You won the toss and chose that one," said Sally "It is too late to complain about the size."

"Just help me get some of these books out, then," said Susan. "I have no room for all of them."

Progress slowed down, as they were looking at each book to see if it would go with Nancy or whether they should look after it for a while. They were quite happy to look after any clothes that had not been actually earmarked; in the past they always looked forward to hand-me-downs when Nancy got new clothes. Sally was particularly good at altering clothes to make them fit. On previous occasions dresses had been eagerly shortened before Nancy decided that perhaps she did want them after all.

"I can't possibly take all these books," said Nancy, "some of them belong to the school anyway".

"I can't carry them all the way to the school, it is too far," said Susan.

"Ask Charlie to carry them for you," said Sally. "I am sure he won't mind."

"I can't ask Charlie to carry my books," said Susan "what will people think?"

"The same as they think when you play kiss chase," said Sally "they already think that you are a forward little hussy."

"I never play kiss chase, the boys always run after the girls anyway, there is nothing I can do," said Susan.

"You always let Charlie catch you," said Sally.

"No I don't. I just can't run as fast as you," said Susan, blushing.

"Everyone's talking about you," said Sally.

"You're always whispering with Kit," said Susan and it was Sally's turn to blush.

Richard and Kit came to the back door with the horse and cart, and Sally hoped they had not been overheard.

"Is that all that there is to go on the cart?" asked Richard.

"There's some more as well," said Susan. "We wouldn't want Nancy to miss any of her possessions."

Kit stolidly loaded a large trunk; bags and bundles were fitted around it, wherever there was space.

"This is very important, it's Benjie's," whispered Susan, handing her father a small box. "Charlie was looking after it for him."

She needn't have worried about Kit listening, because he had already worked out what was going on.

"This little package is for Hamish," said Richard. "It is very important that Benjie gives it to him, rather than you."

"Why should Benjie give it to him?" asked Nancy.

"Benjie will be his 'first foot', their first visitor of the New Year, it will bring good luck if the first foot is a dark man bringing coal and whisky," said Richard.

"I'll make sure he gets it," said Nancy

"Is that all?" asked Richard. "I need to start tying everything down and protect it from the weather."

"Nearly," said Susan, handing over a large globe.

"That won't fit anywhere," said Nancy "It must go back to the school."

"There is room in that corner," said Susan. "And there are all these slates."

"Benjie won't want to see any more of those," said Nancy, "but I could keep a few in case I have to run a dame school." She realized that she had no idea what she would be doing for the rest of her life; this thought was scary but exciting. She said fond farewells to her father and Susan, shook Kit's hand, and got up on the cart. Sally was still looking for things that might have been missed.

"Where's the dowry?" asked Sally "I didn't see it."

"Would you recognize it?" asked Nancy.

"What does it look like?" asked Sally.

"I'm driving it," said Nancy.

"I am setting Nancy and Benjie up in business so the horse and cart are Nancy's dowry," said Richard.

It dawned on Sally that their sister was going to leave them and live somewhere else, and she went over to the cart and clung to her.

"Don't cry, the tears will shrink my new gown," said Nancy, but she said it kindly and Sally smiled through her tears. "No, Susan, don't bring that ink, it will get everywhere, everything has been fastened down, and there is nowhere to put anything else."

"You had better have this, then," said Susan, handing Nancy a well-used cane. "I can't take that into school for you, and it might get into the wrong hands."

"Those poor little children in your dame school may be in for a bit of a surprise," said Richard, trying to keep the parting as light as possible. "Do you think you can drive as far as the meeting place?"

"Yes, I have been practising," said Nancy. "But how will you manage without Spot and the cart?"

"I took the opportunity to order a new cart," said Richard. "And the ostlers have chosen a younger, faster horse for me."

"Who will look after us now you are going?" wailed Sally as she rushed up to kiss Nancy.

"We'll look after each other," said Susan. "Now go and get your things off MY bed!"

Nancy had tears in her eyes as she set off; she would really miss her kind father and noisy sisters. Strangely enough, she would especially miss her sisters arguing. The conversation became fainter and fainter.

"Your bed is much bigger than mine!"

"No it isn't. Anyway it squeaks very loudly."

"So does Nancy's. That's why they had to use the hayloft."

"That is ENOUGH you two. Get inside out of the cold and put the kettle on."

"Anybody want any toast?"

She turned the corner and couldn't hear anymore; for the first time in her life there was silence, not the hard won silence of the classroom, but real silence.

***

Nancy sat on the cart at the crossroads, trying to look as inconspicuous as she could with a loaded cart and a piebald horse. She was glad it was dark; this elopement would have been impossible in summer. There was no sign of Benjie; she felt that he should have been waiting. Could he have changed his mind? She saw a large dark figure go up the lane to the right; she hoped nobody had seen her, and she particularly hoped that it wasn't Frank.

In front of her, much further around the corner, she could almost see the ale house and the New Year revelers. Martha's gang would be there for most of the night, drinking because there was food laid on, a bit of a party. Hopefully it would keep everyone occupied and the gang would not see Benjie slip away. He must have been delayed, late back from the quarry. Could anything have happened to him? Was he all right?

To the left was the long lonely lane leading to the ramshackle set of buildings where Martha and her gang lived. Could Benjie still be there? She wondered if she should move up the lane, but he may come from the ale house direction in the meantime. And she was not sure where to start looking for him. And if he had changed his mind, and she went searching for him, she would be a laughing stock.

Benjie could be injured, or even dead! He could have had an accident in the quarry. Nancy thought that it was more likely that Benjie was just waiting his chance to get away and she chased away her gloomy thoughts. She had to stay where she was, it had been agreed, and she was hidden as much as possible.

Behind her was the lane leading up to her home. Her former home, she corrected. Where did she belong now? What could be keeping Benjie? She shivered and waited.

27 THE ALE HOUSE

The kitchen at the back of the surgery had been tidied up for Christmas, but was getting back to normal. Books and papers were making their way back onto the table, and the holly competed with the cobwebs for space on the mantelpiece. Benjie had not arrived as expected, and Charlie was fretting.

"Benjie is late, he should be here by now," said Charlie.

"Could he have gone straight to the crossroads?" asked Tom.

"He said he would come here first," said Charlie.

"The revels will be starting, we will be needed at the ale house soon," said Tom, "we have a job to do; I expect we will be kept busy tonight."

"I will wait here in case Benjie arrives," said William, "I am getting a bit old for revels. I prefer the fireside and an easy life."

Tom packed his bag with things he would need for patching up minor injuries, and prepared to set out into the cold. He wondered how old you had to be to look forward to a night by the fireside; he felt quite close to it now. Charlie, on the other hand, was very eager for revels.

"You could stay in if you wanted," said Tom, "you have worked hard this week".

"I volunteered for wheelbarrow duty," said Charlie. "I hear that the food is very good at New Year; it is a pity that people sometimes throw it at each other. Adam says it doesn't taste so good after it has been scraped off the wall."

"You might as well make yourself useful and carry the bag, then," said Tom. "It could be a long night."

There was no sign of Benjie or Ox in the ale house; Charlie thought they must be late back from the quarry but Tom noticed that the other quarrymen were there. Frank swaggered in, followed by the remaining members of Martha's gang.

Martha was not with them; she would be at home enjoying her laudanum. Tom had given her very good measure that afternoon, mainly by accident because he was very preoccupied. Martha had not given him a chance to make the correction, paid him quickly without arguing, and hurried out.

Frank looked as if he expected a fight, and the quarrymen appeared as if they would oblige him.

"It's no use looking for Benjie," said Frank.

"Where is he?" asked the quarry foreman.

"Benjie has been locked up, for telling lies again. Got us into trouble. Said we shouldn't have sent young Caleb to work in the quarry," said Frank.

"No more you shouldn't," said the quarry foreman.

"You should look after your workers better," said Frank. "Not our fault."

"I saw the quarry and the workers with my own eyes," said Tom. "Benjie didn't need to tell me anything."

"Benjie is a liar, he gets that from that gypsy mother of his," said Frank. "Martha is always telling us."

"Benjie tells the truth," said the quarry foreman.

"No New Year revels for Benjie, he is locked up and the key is in my pocket," said Frank. He threw a stool at Tom's head, but Tom unexpectedly caught it by the leg and earned himself a round of applause.

The foreman threw the nearest plate at Frank, which was a signal for everyone to settle a few scores. Tom and George joined in, in spite of Arthur's protests. Adam and Charlie grabbed large platefuls of food, but retreated to a safe corner, complaining that it had all started early this year.

Most of the food was on wooden or metal plates, but there was enough second rate pottery to make a satisfying noise when it hit the wall and slid down. One of Martha's gang threw a tankard towards Tom, but he slipped on the messy floor and the tankard missed him. The tankard sailed on and hit Frank, the only man who could match Tom in height. When the missile hit Frank on the head, he went out like a light. The quarry foreman was getting into the swing of things and threw a very large glass dish containing a trifle. The trifle was usually served in an earthenware dish and Arthur resolved to have a word with the girls in the kitchen. His regular staff knew better than to use a glass dish, but he did not think that anyone would remember who had been responsible.

The lobbing of the trifle signalled the end of the fighting, as everyone was avoiding the splinters of glass that were scattered everywhere. The jam of the trifle went far and wide, making the carnage look much worse than it was. With Frank unconscious the quarrymen held the balance of power and they wanted to get their supper. The table was still standing, which was unusual, and some of the hardier men salvaged some of the food. The floor was littered with tankards, food and furniture; over the top was a scattering of glass and pottery shards. There was blood and jam everywhere, including the walls.

Tom moved towards Frank, to sneak the key out of his pocket and rescue Benjie before Frank woke up, but it was difficult with so many of the gang between Tom and the key. There was an uneasy truce while some of the debris was swept into a corner and chairs were replaced, and Tom did not want to disturb it. Frank looked as if he would be asleep for a while, and there would be an opportunity later.

Tom started treating the injuries, hoping to inch his way closer to Frank. One of the men had a dislocated shoulder; the treatment, the yells and the swearing provided great entertainment before the unfortunate man was sent home in the wheelbarrow. Tom worked his way through the minor injuries, without the help of Charlie. He wondered if the lad was still eating somewhere, and then remembered that he had seen Adam and Charlie pushing the wheelbarrow out.

After sorting out the cuts and bruises, Tom turned his attention to Frank. The best way to deal with him would be to get him carried home without waking him up first, that could wait until the wheelbarrow returned; there would not be many volunteers to take Frank home. Adam and Charlie certainly couldn't manage it; Frank was far too heavy for them. Where was Kit? Ox? Richard?

Ostensibly checking for injuries, Tom very carefully looked for the key but there was nothing in Frank's pockets, cap or boots and he wondered where it had gone. He searched for the key on the floor, hoping that it wasn't in the pile of glass and debris swept into the corner. Perhaps the key was in the usual place after all; Charlie had told him where it was kept.

Tom was hesitating, wondering what to do. He could go up the lane and try to rescue Benjie, but could he be sure he wouldn't be followed? Would he make matters worse and draw attention to what was happening? And there would be work for him to do in the ale house; if he deserted his post it would be difficult to face Arthur later.

The fighting might break out again at any minute, and he would be needed, especially when midnight came and they would be singing Auld Lang Syne and remembering insults from previous years. Adam came in, and wanted a quiet word with Tom outside.

"Charlie's gone on an errand, he said you would know all about it," said Adam. "He was very mysterious, said he was going to fetch something out of the storeroom, and he knew where to find the key."

"We've run out of arnica, there is none for the next lot of bruises," said Tom, being careful in case he was overheard. "I asked him to pick some up." So that was what had happened to the key! When had Charlie learnt to pick pockets?

"Charlie said that he hoped he wouldn't be long. Is it all right to wait until he gets back before I take anyone else home? It takes two of us, but Kit can usually manage on his own," said Adam. "I'd expected him here tonight; he is missing the food."

"There's only one casualty left to take home," said Tom "and he is much too heavy for you, or even the two of you. It will take Richard, Ox and Kit to lift him in and two of them to take him home. He is fine where he is for the time being," said Tom. "I think you should go and see if there is some food left."

Tom needed to stall for as long as possible, while Benjie got away; the longer Frank stayed asleep, the better.

28 THE PRISONER

Benjie could only hope that Nancy had tired of waiting and gone back home. Perhaps she would realize what had happened and Richard would release him from this prison. But the humiliation of being released by Nancy's friends and family! And someone might get hurt and he couldn't bear that. Not on his account, he wasn't worth it.

Benjie felt that he just wasn't good enough for Nancy, and her family had been so helpful to him. Already there had been so many favours he couldn't begin to repay. In contrast, his grandmother caused much of the trouble in the town, good lads were hurt, or worse, and there was nothing he could do about it; he thought about Caleb again and almost wept.

If only he could be released in time to make sure that Nancy was all right; waiting at the crossroads was worse than waiting at the altar – at least in a church she would have been safe. He was so wrapped up in his thoughts that he didn't hear the key turning in the lock. He expected Frank coming to taunt him, and backed into a corner to make it easier to defend himself. But it wasn't Frank, or Richard, the figure silhouetted in the moonlight was much smaller.

"Is that you, Charlie?" asked Benjie.

"Who else would it be?" said Charlie. "We will have to be quick, and quiet."

"Is Nancy all right?" asked Benjie, as he started moving. He felt very stiff; perhaps he was bruised.

"Yes, she is waiting, she knows you have been delayed. She is still at the crossroads, so that people won't notice her," said Charlie. "Hurry up, Nancy won't wait for ever."

"I will need to collect my things from your shop," said Benjie. They were talking in whispers as they hurried along.

"All loaded on the cart for you," said Charlie, "except for this." He handed

Benjie a bag of coins. "You left me some money to look after."

"Not as much as this," said Benjie, feeling the weight of it.

"We were lucky with some of our bets," said Charlie, "good odds on the home team for the quoits game. No one else rated them but I knew we would win."

"Thank you so much," said Benjie," I can't believe that I have been rescued by someone in my own family."

"We are not out of the woods yet."

"Where's Frank?"

"He got knocked out during the food fight; they said that the scuffle started early this year. Frank could wake up any minute, don't hang about."

"And our grandmother?" asked Benjie, quickening his footsteps.

"At home, hopefully asleep," said Charlie. They both looked around, just in case.

The crossroads was in sight at last but a very large man came out of the opposite lane, and hurried towards the town.

"Was that Frank?" asked Charlie, scared, as they flattened themselves into the wall so as not to be seen.

"I think it was Ox," said Benjie "He must have been to see Caleb's mother. I can't believe that I haven't been to see her, I feel terrible."

"You haven't time, now," said Charlie, as they finally reached the crossroads.

"Are you all right, Nancy? I am so sorry I was late; I couldn't help it. You should have gone home, I am not worth waiting for," said Benjie.

"Please get up on the cart," said Nancy, "never mind making friends with the horse, you can do that later."

"I need to get changed into my best clothes, I can't get married in my working clothes," said Benjie.

"Get up on the cart," said Nancy "it is time to go, you can get changed later."

"Thank you so much, Charlie, for all that you have done, I can never repay you," said Benjie.

"We are family, and you have given me so much already. I am so lucky to be working for the doctors," said Charlie. "I think Miss Nancy is getting a little impatient."

"Get up on the cart NOW" said Nancy. "Let's get out of here."

It wasn't quite that easy, Benjie was more bruised than he thought, so he had to be pushed by Charlie and pulled by Nancy. Then he insisted on driving, and had to change places. The progress was a little uneven for a while, as Benjie redistributed his money between his pockets, his boots and one or two of the bags.

**

They settled down to a steady pace on the Carlisle road; the signposts reassured them that they were going in the right direction.

"I am so unbelievably happy to be with you," said Nancy, hoping the delay would not cause them any difficulty.

"It is wonderful to be with you, I can't believe that we will be together always," said Benjie. He was not beholden to Richard or Tom for his escape; his own cousin, Charlie, had helped him. And Charlie would not have been there if it had not been for Benjie's own efforts in finding him an apprenticeship with the doctors. And the money was a bonus he hadn't expected. Benjie wondered if he would have time to count some of it next time the moon came out.

"Once we get past Carlisle it is only a few miles to Gretna. I think Hamish lives in the first house we get to," said Nancy.

"That's right, I remember some of the quoits team saying. I hope we don't disturb their Hogmanay party," said Benjie.

"Weddings are their job; Gretna people rely on the English like us for their livelihood. But you might be their first foot, though I doubt it now as we are late."

"Have we anything to give them?"

"You must go in first, and give them coal and whisky," said Nancy, handing them to him.

"The whisky will come in useful to keep out the cold. I'm sure they won't miss a drop."

"Hamish will send someone for the anvil priest, and then we can get married right away. No-one will be able to separate us; we will be together forever."

Benjie thought that was a wonderful prospect, but wondered how they would make a living.

"You didn't ask about the dowry."

"I didn't like to."

"You are driving it," said Nancy. "The horse and cart is our dowry; we can use it to start our new carting business."

Benjie couldn't believe his luck, he knew all about horses and carts, with a lot of practice over the years. He would be earning his living, instead of being a kept man.

"Where would we live?" asked Benjie. It was the first time he had thought that far ahead.

"We would go back, I suppose," said Nancy but she would have preferred a new start.

"There seem to be plenty of carters at home, maybe we could set up in Gretna," said Benjie. Scotland was another country, so it seemed further from Martha's gang.

"That would be nice," said Nancy, wondering how she would fit in. All her life she felt that she needed to be in control of everything; but how would she manage in a foreign country?

"Charlie said they were desperately short of carters where Tom's brother lives in Hilltop," said Benjie.

"I am not surprised," said Nancy, shivering. "They have worse weather than we do." The town at Hilltop was made up of a collection of villages, very different from home.

The night was cold but fine; ice was forming on the road, so Benjie kept a careful steady pace, in spite of Nancy worrying about being followed.

"I don't suppose you have anything to eat, have you? I haven't eaten for hours," asked Benjie hopefully.

Nancy rummaged in one of the bags and found bread and cheese thoughtfully provided by Sally. Benjie ate as they travelled, as Nancy said they should not stop. Benjie thought that it would be a good idea to have something to eat, in case they needed a nip of whisky later.

29 THE REVELS

Everything was fairly quiet at the ale house, some of the women and older people had ventured out of the kitchen but were ready to go back if necessary. Tom was just outside the door to see who was coming and going, but he kept a wary eye on Frank in case he woke up.

Ox came in and noticed that food was already on the walls and that people were warily stepping around his brother Frank on the floor. Tom felt that if the fighting started again, the balance of power would be in Frank's favour, but he need not have worried. Ox said that he was sorry he had missed the fun, but made eating and drinking a priority.

A few minutes later Richard came in. He had left Kit at home, to protect the girls if it was needed so he volunteered to take Kit's place on wheelbarrow duty if necessary. There was enough muscle power now to take Frank home, but they decided to let sleeping bullies lie.

Charlie arrived just before midnight, with more medical supplies in case they were needed, and William had come with him, to see the New Year in. Richard and Tom were very relieved that Nancy and Benjie were on their way, but watched Frank and Ox just in case. There was no sign of Martha, and she was not expected to arrive.

***

The clock started striking midnight, and everyone gathered to sing. Charlie had stationed himself hopefully near the mistletoe, wondering if grown-ups still played kiss chase. They all linked and sang, Arthur and his father Edward had fine voices and could carry a tune well enough to help everyone else. Edward even knew the second verse of Auld Lang Syne; they were very proud of him.

Everything went well until the last chorus, when they had to remain linked and surge into the middle of the room. There were too many people, not enough space, and definitely not enough coordination. Once one person slipped on the trifle, it put everybody off balance, half a dozen broke away, staggered towards the corner, and fell heavily on top of Frank, swearing and laughing.

Frank woke up with a roar, wondering what had happened, and why the food fight had stopped. He picked up a large plate of pies and hurled it at the quarry foreman, who ducked, the pies ricocheting off the wall. Some people picked them up and either ate them or threw them back half-heartedly but nobody's aim was very good.

Frank looked at Ox, who felt that something was expected of him so he picked up a large dish of rum butter and hefted it. Everyone cringed; would Ox throw it at the quarrymen who he worked with? Or would he throw it at his brother who expected his loyalty? Which side was Ox on?

Ox was on his own side, and he took another look at the rum butter, dipped a grubby finger in, and tasted it. After he dipped his finger in a second time, he decided that food was much too good to waste. Ox sat down to concentrate better, and was soon scooping large handfuls of rum butter. Nobody else fancied eating anything, so Arthur and the staff started clearing away.

Frank got to his feet, looking around belligerently, so the quarry foreman and two of his men got to their feet and waited. Ox was busy, the rest of Martha's gang looked tired, so Frank decided to pick on Tom.

"What are you still doing here?" asked Frank, loudly.

"Just doing my job," said Tom. There was a murmur of approval from the crowd.

"Shouldn't you be with Nancy? Running away to get married?" asked Frank.

"That's what I heard. You are leaving it a bit late," said Arthur. "Dr. Jarvis and Charlie can take over now, and patch people up."

"Someone might get cut from one of your pies," said some joker.

"Have you left her in the lurch?" jeered Frank. "Shame on you!"

"She was waiting at the crossroads, I saw her," said Ox.

"Nancy has gone now," said the joker.

"Back home on her own?" asked Frank.

"On the Carlisle road; she had someone with her," said the joker.

"Missed your chance there," said Frank.

"Looked like young Charlie," said the joker.

"He is surprisingly popular with the women," said Tom, trying to buy more time.

"No, Charlie is here," said Arthur. Charlie could not say anything because his face was full of pie.

They all wondered who could have been on the cart with Nancy. There were guesses of this person or that, trying to account for everybody. Tom, Charlie and William all joined in the speculations, desperately hoping that time would not run out. Frank wondered about Benjie. It was known that Benjie was courting some girl; he had asked permission to marry. He wondered whether it was possible but he checked his pocket and the key was still there.

The door opened suddenly and Martha Armstrong stood in front of them.

"Benjie's gone! Frank, did you let him out?" she waved her stick at Frank and he cringed.

"No, Ma'am. I did as you said, Ma'am. Someone must have stolen the key," said Frank, but he knew that the key was in his pocket.

"Don't just stand there, get after him, he can't have got far," said Martha, moving forward with her stick. A ripple of laughter went around the room, at Frank's expense.

"Right away, Ma'am," said Frank.

"I would advise against it, after a bump on the head like that. You would be better to rest for an hour or two before you do anything," said William.

"Rubbish! You don't need mollycoddling. I have even brought the horse, so you have no excuse," said Martha. "Get a move on."

Utterly humiliated, Frank did as he was told, but at least he knew which direction to take. He would return with honour if he brought Benjie back, one way or another.

"I want my property back," said Martha. "I spent money bringing that lad up and he hasn't paid me back yet. He has to work for me until he is twenty-one."

But Frank had gone.

***

There was confusion as everybody worked out what was happening. Tom decided to get Thunderbolt saddled so that he could follow Frank and make sure that Nancy and Benjie came to no harm. Richard arranged to borrow a horse, but thought this might take a little while to organize. Ox was still busy with the rum butter, and refused to join in the chase in spite of Martha's orders. He knew he would be in trouble in the morning but didn't care anymore.

None of the other men were in a fit state to do much, so Arthur supplied more ale and organized the clearing up as best he could. Everyone said it was the best New Year for ages. Arthur made sure that Martha's jug was kept full, and she obliged by falling asleep in the corner and snoring loudly.

***

Tom stood impatiently in the stables while Thunderbolt was saddled, worrying whether he would arrive too late to save Benjie and Nancy. He

135

wondered how far they had managed to travel; perhaps they were beyond Carlisle already and there would be no problem. Once they got to Gretna, Hamish and his friends would look after them. Otherwise Frank would overtake the cart; Spot was faster than Star, but not if he had a cart to pull. Tom hoped Thunderbolt would live up to his name; he was not a carthorse like the others.

Tom was really glad that Benjie had talked him into buying a reliable horse that would not have its own agenda; it was not a good time for a horse to be chasing the mares. Tom had lots of recent riding practice; he winced when he remembered the ride to Hilltop. The ostlers seemed a bit befuddled, and Tom had to lend a hand here and there to hurry them on.

If Tom caught up with Frank before he got to the cart, Tom could distract him enough for the others to get away. There was a stout cudgel in the saddlebags; he couldn't stop Frank, but he could slow him down. But if Benjie saw him, he would not allow Tom to fight Frank on his own. Could Tom and Benjie overpower Frank between them? They had to, right was on their side. Wasn't it?

They could at least hold on until Richard arrived, but he might take a while for him to catch up. There was only one horse available for Richard to borrow, and Dobbin just wanted to sleep.

30 THE CHASE

Nancy cuddled up to Benjie and wrapped her cloak around both of them to keep warm; it was exciting and romantic to elope to Gretna Green, but also cold and uncomfortable.

"Can we go any faster?" she asked.

"There is ice on the road, it is better to be safe," he said.

"Are you sure about the ice?"

"It's treacherous. I don't tell you how to teach your class."

Nancy felt that he had a point, but would feel much happier when they arrived at their destination. The moon came out from behind a cloud and she could see the road in front of her. When they went over the top of the next hill, she could see the river shining, far in the distance, so they must be getting closer to the border.

Nancy wondered what the future would hold for them; she wondered if she could easily get used to being a carter's wife instead of a schoolteacher. She would look after Benjie, and they would live in their own little house. She let her mind rest on the thought of how this house would be, imagining furniture and china, and she decided that it would be nicer than Jeannie and George's house.

It was more difficult to imagine living in a place where she knew nobody. At home she could not turn a corner without seeing friends, neighbours and relatives and the streets were full of children that she had taught in her class. She had a social position and respect because of her father's standing in the town. Without family, they would have to make their own way, earn their own respect, and it could take a long time.

Nancy brought her mind back to the present; she could hear the wind, the rattling of the cart and the clip clop of the horse's hooves. She heard the echo of the hooves for the first time and thought that it was a very lonely place.

"Benjie, what'll it be like living in a strange place where nobody knows us?"

"Hamish and his team know us, they have known your father for years. Don't worry, they'll give us a good welcome."

"And if it is Hilltop?" Nancy shivered.

"Tom's brother and uncles live there and my cousin works for Tom. That makes us practically family."

"Your family, not mine."

"My family is yours," said Benjie, "with one exception. I wouldn't wish my grandmother on anybody."

"We have each other," said Nancy "I'll stop worrying."

"Can you hear anything?"

"I can hear the wind, the cart and the horse. The church bells have all stopped now, they must have been ringing the New Year in."

"Nothing else?"

"An echo of Spot's hooves on the road."

"I don't think that is an echo," said Benjie "I think there is another horse following us."

Nancy looked around at the road behind her, but could see nothing. The echo seemed a bit louder than it had been.

"I can't see anyone," she said. But she wasn't quite so sure that the road was empty.

"It may be something and nothing," said Benjie, "but can you keep looking, please? Whenever the moon comes out, or when you can see more of the road."

Nancy shrugged off the cloak on her left hand side so that she could turn and scan the horizon.

"Which horse did you think it was?"

"It was a bit 'dot and carry', like Star. If Frank is following, he could catch up before we get to Gretna; the cart slows us down."

"Star could slip on the ice and throw Frank," said Nancy "Especially if Frank is not as careful as you."

"I hope so, as long as Star isn't hurt. Frank has ill-treated that horse for years, it is time he got his own back." But he didn't sound convinced.

They reached a dip in the road and there seemed to be something coming over the brow of the hill. A few seconds later, Nancy could make out the shape of a horse and rider. She suddenly felt very scared, and her heart was thumping so loudly she could not hear anything else.

"There is a horse and rider, going very unevenly. The horse has a white blaze on his face, shaped like a star and the man looks big and heavy," she said.

"Frank on Star," said Benjie "we just have to keep going and hope for the best."

Frank applied the whip; Star slipped and righted himself. They seemed to be inching closer to Benjie and Nancy. The following hooves were louder, and the sound seemed to change slightly.

"Do you hear anyone else, or just us and Frank?" asked Benjie.

"I am not sure," said Nancy "Maybe there is someone else, come to rescue us." She couldn't think who it could be. It was more likely to be more of Martha's gang, or a stranger, or even a highwayman.

Nancy had a last look back when they reached the top of the next hill, afraid of what she might see. There was another horse and rider just coming over the brow of the previous hill, some distance away.

"Did you see who it was?" asked Benjie.

"A pale horse," said Nancy. She shivered. According to the Bible, death always rode on a pale horse.

Benjie turned and saw the other rider and the tall awkward looking rider was unmistakable.

"Dr. Tom," he said. "If he is here there may be others on the way. We just have to hang on and hope for the best. I still have to be careful and make sure that the horse does not slip." But he quickened his pace.

Nancy and Benjie went over the brow of the hill and could see no one. Frank was gaining on them; they could only hope that Tom was gaining on Frank. By the time they got to the dip in the road they could see Frank, he was yelling and whipping the horse.

Nancy worked free of the cloak so that she could deal with any attempts to board the cart on her side; she would do anything to buy them time before the rescuers got there. Frank must not hurt Benjie anymore.

Benjie kept going; he had a horsewhip in his hand but was not planning to use it on Spot. He would rather deal with Frank than be rescued again, but he was not in a position to be picky.

Frank caught up with them when they were half way down the hill, threatening and yelling at them to stop. Frank attempted to force the cart into the ditch, but Benjie managed to keep them upright and on the road. Tom was just coming over the top of the hill, too far away to help them. If only they could hold on.

Frank made his first attempt to board the cart on Benjie's side, but was pushed away with the whip. A few minutes later, Nancy was terrified to find Frank alongside her side of the cart. It would take too long to get the whip from Benjie, so she picked up the cane to defend herself. She slashed at Frank but he still kept going.

Frank stood up in the stirrups, kept one hand on the reins, and reached over to the cart to climb on to it. Nancy brought the cane down on his knuckles as hard as she could, he yelped and let go, a look of pained surprise on his face. Star slipped on the ice again, stumbled and nearly fell. Frank was caught off balance, fell between Spot and the cart, and the wheel ran over him.

Benjie brought the cart to a halt; he and Nancy got down and saw that Frank was lying very still on the road.

"What have I done?" wailed Nancy.

"You did what you had to do to defend yourself," said Benjie, shakily.

"I saw what happened," said Tom, as he rode up. He checked to see whether Frank was just stunned, but it was all as they suspected.

"I killed a man! I hit him and now he is dead," said Nancy in a trembling voice.

"It wasn't you, I ran over him with the cart!" said Benjie, willing to take the blame.

"The horse slipped on the ice and threw Frank, the fall probably killed him," said Tom, authoritatively." I will know better in the morning; it is too dark to see now. It looks as if Frank lost his balance because he was trying to board the cart."

Star was innocently eating grass by the side of the road; Tom made a grab for his reins. Star moved a little further on, and started eating grass again. Tom tried again and Star ran off; they did not see which direction he took but the horse did not appear to be going home. Spot wanted to take the opportunity to do the same, and it took all Benjie's skill to hold him.

"I murdered Frank!" wailed Nancy as she clung to Tom. "What will happen now? Will they hang me?"

"It was an accident, the horse threw him," said Tom.

"They might not hang me if it's self-defence," said Nancy, sobbing.

"No, but they might hang Benjie if they thought he ran over Frank on purpose," said Tom. "Benjie would admit causing Frank's death, if he thought it would save you."

Nancy went very quiet; she was shaking and shivering. She had put Benjie in danger again. Life beyond the limits of their little town seemed completely unpredictable and Nancy felt, for the first time in her life, that she had no control over events at all.

Benjie came back, after securing Spot so that the cart did not move; he wrapped the cloak around Nancy and pulled her to him.

"What do I have to do?" asked Nancy.

"Frank tried to get on to the cart on your side. The horse slipped and threw him. He fell onto the road and under the cart. Neither of you hit him," said Tom, spelling it out slowly.

"But the marks?" asked Nancy.

"Will not show compared with his other injuries," said Tom.

"But you will have to tell the authorities I confessed," said Nancy.

"Not if you are my patient," said Tom. "Benjie, your wife does not look well."

"She is overwrought, "said Benjie, with a smile, "imagining things."

"I advise my patient to try and get some rest," said Tom.

"What do we do now?" asked Benjie.

"Keep on going to Gretna. I will let you know if you are needed at the inquest," said Tom.

They were about to set off when a horse and rider came over the top of the hill, which put Nancy in a panic again.

"So you finally got here," said Tom.

"Dobbin is getting old and slow," said Richard. "What happened here?"

"Frank tried to get on to the cart on Nancy's side. The horse slipped and threw him and he fell on the road and under the cart," said Tom.

"I am not surprised," said Richard. "The way Frank treated that horse, it has borne a grudge for years. Where is it now?"

"Gone," said Benjie.

"Best way," said Richard. "Get off to Gretna, Tom and I will look after things here."

Nancy felt absolutely shattered as she cuddled up to Benjie on the cart. She just couldn't take in what had happened. She hated to tell a lie, or part of one, but would do as she was told rather than put Benjie in any sort of danger.

31 THE DAWN

Tom and Richard rode slowly back to the town to break the news. The night was cold and completely silent except for the wind. The sky was beginning to get lighter, and they could see the outline of the fells in the distance. They were both thinking about the casualty on the road, and how it would affect their lives.

"Is that really what happened?" asked Richard.

"I saw it all, I just couldn't catch up before Frank tried to get on to the cart. He fell before Benjie and Nancy needed to defend themselves," said Tom.

"Any contributing factors?" asked Richard.

"Frank was tired, and sustained a blow to the head earlier in the evening; he was riding a bad tempered horse much too fast on an icy road. I will make my full report in the morning, when it is daylight; at the moment it looks like accidental death," said Tom, as they set off to break the news.

"Or Act of God?" said Richard.

"Nancy and Benjie needed some divine help," said Tom. "We would not have been in time."

Tom and Richard were both very quiet as they thought about what could have happened. Tom also thought about Nancy, unsure and vulnerable as she clung to him on the road, he had never seen that side of her before, and wondered if it would have made a difference if he had. Tom had always loved Nancy, but she always wanted everything on her terms and he was very cautious about making changes. Perhaps if either of them had been more patient, things would have turned out differently.

Tom wondered what would have happened to Benjie if Nancy had not whisked him off to Gretna. He had never heard of an elopement where the girl took charge, but it was typical Nancy. He realized that he would miss her, but at least his mother would stop nagging him about marriage, for a while at least.

"They will be safe now."

"It might help if we go slowly; give them time to get wed at Gretna before Martha sends anyone else."

"Dobbin doesn't go quickly at any time," said Richard, "not like your fine horse. Dobbin is old and tired, at least I think it is just Dobbin."

"Benjie chose Thunderbolt for me," said Tom "but he said that Dobbin always knew his way to the ale house."

"That is always useful."

"Benjie found an excellent apprentice for me as well," said Tom as he realized that he would miss Benjie, who had been a good friend to him.

"And that led to Charlie telling me about Kit," said Richard, "an asset to the forge and the quoits team," said Tom.

They made their way slowly back, stopping to admire the spectacular sunrise and smoke a pipe or two.

"Nancy is a good lass, you know, it's just that some men don't like to be mithered too much," said Richard

"Even for their own good."

"I don't think Benjie will mind."

"I think he will be used to it," said Tom. He thought of his own comfortable home, with three bachelors who never mithered each other. Nancy was the love of his life, but would have been very difficult to live with.

***

Tom and Richard were surprised to see quite a few people waiting for them when they got back.

"What have you to report?" asked William, who was sitting near the dying fire. Charlie was leaning against him, and had fallen asleep.

"A marriage," said Tom, solemnly, "and I am sorry to report that there has been a death."

"I'm pleased to announce the engagement of my daughter, Nancy, to Mr. Benjamin Armstrong," said Richard. "They will be married by now, Benjie is a lovely lad and I am proud to have him for a son-in-law."

A round of applause went round the room, many people saying that they knew all the time and wondering where the young couple would live.

"Who died?" asked Ox. He was sitting at the table with the quarry gang, next to the foreman.

"I'm sorry to say that your brother Frank died accidentally this morning," said Tom.

"How did it happen?" asked Ox. "I know he had been told to set off after Benjie – what went wrong?"

"What about my horse?" asked Ma, suddenly awake. She sat surrounded by her gang.

"I saw him try to board Nancy's cart and his horse seemed to slip as he was moving over. Frank fell on to the road, and the back wheel of the cart ran over him. It looks as if the fall killed him, but I will know for sure when I have done my report for the inquest," said Tom.

"WHAT ABOUT THE HORSE?" shouted Martha.

"It ran off, we couldn't catch it," said Tom.

"Stolen!" said Martha.

"What would Benjie and Nancy want with your horse? They have a much better one; nobody stole your horse, it just ran off," said Tom.

"How can you worry about your horse?" asked Ox. "My brother is dead. He worked hard for you all these years and you just don't care!"

"I can easily get more people, but that horse cost a lot of money. I want it found. NOW!" said Martha. One by one her gang remembered work they had to do, and started drifting away. It was cold, and they had no idea which direction the horse took.

"Just you then, Ox. What are you waiting for? Off you go!" ordered Martha.

"I will go to fetch my brother's body, but I am not chasing after that horse," said Ox.

"In that case you are fired," said Martha. "Good riddance."

"I have had an offer to work at the quarry and live at the barracks," said Ox." An extra half penny a day and everything so I don't need to work for you anymore."

"Don't expect me to pay for Frank's funeral," said Martha. They all knew that she never paid for funerals.

"I have no money," said Ox.

"I can lend you the money and stop it out of your wages until it is paid," said the foreman and Ox looked at him gratefully.

"I think we can do the funeral at a reduced rate," said the carpenter. "I wanted to give my lad a practice coffin to do – a sort of apprentice piece. This will be a good test for him."

"I will see you, doctor, at the inquest," said Martha and swept out.

Tom's father, John, had been listening to all that was going on.

"Before you go, lad, your mother and I would like a little word," said John. Tom realized he had been cornered.

Tom had not noticed that his parents had waited for him, in a quiet corner with Jeannie and George. As the younger couple left, Tom prepared himself for what his mother might say. He had not actually lied, but he could have told more of the truth so he felt more nervous than when he was getting ready to face Frank.

"How long has this been going on, and why didn't you tell me about Nancy and Benjie?" demanded Sarah.

"Benjie asked for my blessing in the summer and I gave it gladly. But I never tell my patients' secrets," said Tom.

"You may be a grand doctor to everyone else in the town, but you are still my son and I expect consideration and respect from you," said Sarah.

"You have my love and respect but I cannot provide you with information about my patients. I am constrained by my profession, but anyway it would be wrong. My patients need to trust me, otherwise I cannot make a living," said Tom.

"I suppose so," said John.

"But we are entitled to know whether you are planning marriage or not," said Sarah.

"If I plan to get married, I will tell you in good time!" said Tom, sharply.

"I wasn't really trying to push you into marrying Nancy. You just didn't seem to make up your mind and I had got really fond of Nancy. It would have been lovely to have had her in the family," said Sarah.

"You're of age now, I suppose you are entitled to a few secrets," said John. "Maybe you have a mistress hidden away somewhere?"

There was a gasp from Sarah as she realized that Tom might have a mistress without telling his parents.

"My only mistress is my work; as you see she takes up all my time," said Tom as he stood up, ready to go.

"I know you work very hard, and do a good job, everyone says so." said John. "Is Elizabeth really getting better?"

"Her cough has gone and she is putting on weight," said Tom. "She could come home now, but she would be poorly again very quickly if she started working at the mill. If she is consumptive, the mill would make her a lot worse."

"I understand that now," said Sarah. "Elizabeth could stay at home and look after us; we are not so young as we were. We could probably manage without another wage coming in."

"Elizabeth is very keen to come home," said Tom. "I will go up and arrange it if she is well enough. Following recent events, there may be a vacancy for a pupil teacher at the school."

" It's an ill wind," said John.

***

Ox rode with the carpenter and his son in their cart with Tom and William riding alongside; they had to make sure that there would be enough room for the body on the return journey as Frank was a big man. The carpenter's son looked very sorry for himself; he didn't feel ready for the challenge of making such a large coffin.

"I'm really glad of your help this morning," said Tom to William.

"I told Charlie the good news, and took him home to rest. If anyone needs a doctor, they will just have to call out the physician. They won't want to pay his prices for hangover cures, so we'll not lose any custom," said William.

"It's good there are two of us examining the body," said Tom. "It might not be clear exactly how Frank died and I will need your advice."

The road looked more desolate than it had looked the previous night, and Frank's body lay where he had fallen. The carpenter's son held the doctors' horses as they examined the body. The Coroner would need to know whether Frank had broken his neck in the fall, or whether the cart wheel killed him. The cause of death could even have been the blow to his head the previous evening.

If death had been caused by that, then it would be manslaughter. Would anyone remember who threw the tankard? Tom remembered that one of Martha's gang had thrown the tankard at him, and had missed and hit Frank. They would probably all blame each other, and nobody would be sure.

If Frank had been killed instantly from the fall, the verdict would be a straightforward accidental death, but there was more blood on Frank than would be expected and Tom wanted to gloss over one of the factors that contributed to the fall.

The worst possible case would be Frank meeting his death by the cart wheel, but Tom would give evidence that it was impossible for Benjie to stop the cart. It was definitely better that William should write the report, in case Tom was called as a witness, but the Coroner could record the death as manslaughter or even murder if it looked as if it had been done on purpose. Would Ox accept that it had been an accident? Would Martha?

32 THE BORDER

Benjie brought the horse and cart to a grateful standstill outside Hamish's forge; there seemed to be some sort of party going on inside, lots of noise and laughter.

"Have we still got the gifts for Hamish?" asked Benjie.

"One lump of coal, one bottle of whisky," said Nancy, knocking on the door.

"Is there any whisky left?" asked Benjie, counting the money in one of his pockets and being pleasantly surprised.

"A little," she said, knocking on the door again.

"We had to keep out the cold," he said, and they both banged on the door.

"Customers!" yelled Hamish above the racket "Oh, it is Richard's daughter and her child bridegroom. Come in, I have been expecting you."

"No, you must go first," said Nancy, as she pushed Benjie forward.

"Our first foot, and a very lucky one for us. Black hair, black face, black fingernails and a black eye," said Hamish as he accepted the gifts. He looked a little disappointed as he hefted the whisky. "Every little helps, I suppose. Is anyone following you?"

"Not anymore," said Nancy.

"Shaken them off, have you? Well done. Then you can get your breath back before the ceremony and I will send someone to find the anvil priest," said Hamish.

"I need to arrange somewhere to stay," said Benjie, resolving to have a wash as well.

"The inns here are very expensive. Well, holiday makers are our living, we don't have a thriving mill like you," said Hamish "I can offer you a fine hayloft."

Nancy's eyes lit up at the thought of a hayloft; she knew how much fun they could be.

"No haylofts for my wife, she deserves nothing but the best," said Benjie. He didn't like to be called a 'child bridegroom'.

"In that case go to the inn at the end of the lane, it is quiet and they will look after you well," said Hamish, pointing in the opposite direction from the big expensive looking inn across the road.

"Come in, Nancy, my wife will look after you and then you can join the party," said Hamish as Benjie led the horse down the road.

***

The inn was just stirring into life when Benjie arrived and arranged for them to stay there. He spoke to the ostlers and settled the horse in to the stables for a well-deserved rest before he did anything else.

Benjie wondered what had happened to Star, whether he would go back home or break free. Would Martha's gang manage without Star to pull the cart? They would have had to buy another horse soon; it did not look as if Star would last the winter anyway, as he was far too old to do the work they expected of him. Benjie was sure that his grandmother could afford a new horse, with the profit she was making from her workers.

Benjie arranged for some of their luggage to be taken up to the room and asked for a fire to be lit so that it would be warm and cosy for Nancy after their long, cold journey. The room was the fanciest he had seen in his life; it had a big four-poster bed in the middle of it, two chairs and a table, and even a little desk. Benjie was overawed and had great difficulty in washing without making a mess but eventually he was ready in his Sunday best clothes; he could see where Charlie had laboured over the mending.

The money would last for two or three weeks, so Benjie needed to work as soon as possible. If he worked as a labourer, he would only get a boy's wage, and it would not be enough. He must find work as a carter if he wanted to keep Nancy as she deserved but the innkeeper seemed to think that there were too many carters in Gretna already.

Benjie realized that they could have worse problems than finding work. Everything depended on the result of Frank's inquest – if the verdict was unlawful killing, there could be a murder charge. Benjie could not stop the wheel running over Frank, but it might look as if he had done it on purpose. He certainly hadn't intended to do Frank any good.

Even if they hung Benjie for murder tomorrow, he did not regret what he had done; marrying Nancy would make it all worthwhile. But what would happen to her afterwards? She lost more than he did by the elopement; her job, her reputation and her home. He was sure that her father would take her back, but she would not be allowed to teach the children anymore. Perhaps Tom would look after her, once she was a widow.

***

Back at Hamish's the drink was flowing and the music was loud; Nancy was watching the dancing and tapping her foot. It looked a very complicated dance and Benjie was glad they were not expected to join in.

"I've sent my son, Young Hamish, to find the anvil priest for you; he should be here shortly.

"We're very grateful," said Benjie.

"It's our living," said Hamish. "Will you be staying here long?"

"I'd hoped to find work here as a carter," said Benjie "but I've heard that you have a lot of carters here already."

"Lots of young people come in with a horse and cart, and set themselves up in business, or they sell their horse and cart locally, for someone else to do it. Everyone and his grandmother has a horse and cart; we have carters to cobble dogs with!" said Hamish.

"The anvil priest is tipsy, he is lying on Big Mari's floor and won't get up," said Young Hamish as he rushed in.

"Not the first time," said Hamish. "Did he give you anything?"

"Just this," said Young Hamish, handing over an untidy dog-eared book.

"The marriage lines are in here somewhere, I will have to do it myself," said Hamish.

"Will the marriage be legal?" asked Benjie.

"Oh yes, there was a court case about one of my weddings once. The marriage was legal all right. The bride and groom both thought better of it in the morning and had hoped to wriggle out of it but they couldn't. Are you thinking of changing your mind?" asked Hamish.

"Never!" said Benjie.

Hamish called for silence and beckoned the young couple to step forward.

33 THE SNOWSTORM

Nancy had been watching the dancing, fascinated by the eightsome reel. She had never seen such a complicated dance, and they seemed to get into such a muddle, especially the awkward man she had seen at the quoits game. He was always going in the wrong direction, and his feet had a little tangle all of their own.

There was another man that she remembered from the quoits match, who was adding to the confusion by shouting out the wrong instructions. Nancy was amazed that people could get so much fun out of doing something so badly. If she had been at home she would have waded in and sorted them out, but she just felt too tired.

Each dancer had a turn in the middle of a little circle, with another seven people dancing around them in a ring, then the chosen dancer took the opportunity to do their own little dance and show off. She would always remember Awkward doing his little dance to Troublemaker's instructions, and she even stopped worrying about what would happen to herself and Benjie after the wedding.

Nancy had seen Benjie as he came in at the door, looking so handsome in his Sunday best that she fell in love with him all over again. He looked quite the gentleman, the effect only spoiled by a black eye that was starting to close. She saw the other girls turning and whispering to each other, wondering who this new man was. Well, Benjie was spoken for!

***

It was a beautifully simple wedding ceremony; Hamish stood behind the anvil and read the words for them to repeat. Benjie had managed to keep his mother's wedding ring all these years, so they did not need to borrow a ring. He promised to buy her a proper ring of her own, but she was more than happy with the one he had given her because she loved him.

After the ceremony they were invited to stay and enjoy the party, but Benjie asked for them to be excused – they had been travelling all night and were very tired. This amused the company greatly and Nancy felt that she was blushing as they made their way to the inn.

Their room looked good with its warm fire and large inviting four-poster bed. Benjie looked wonderful in his Sunday best, but even better without it as he lay in the bed. She still thrilled to his touch and the sound of his voice; just like she had on the day she first met him. Nancy's last thought before she went to sleep sometime later, was that haylofts were overrated and beds were much better.

***

It was early evening when they woke up; they could hear gales and sleet outside but their room was warm and cosy. Nancy wanted to stay in bed forever, but Benjie thought they should keep their strength up, and went to organize some supper.

Nancy took the opportunity to tidy up some of their belongings, and found her cane under one of the bundles. As she looked at the bloodstains on it, she realized that she never wanted to use a cane ever again. Nancy broke the cane, pushed it into the fire as far as she could, and watched it burn to ash, and wished her crime could disappear as easily as the murder weapon.

Nancy could not help thinking about what she had done, and that last look on Frank's face would be with her for the rest of her life. She wondered how he had felt when he fell and saw the wheel coming towards him. She did not hear Benjie come back into the room.

"You look miles away, my love. What were you thinking about?" asked Benjie.

"What will become of us?" asked Nancy.

"It looks as if there will not be enough work for us in Gretna. We could go back home.".

"Or a new start somewhere else," said Nancy. She was not sure that she could face everybody at home.

"We could go to Hilltop, there is enough work for another carter. Would you mind very much? The locals say that the weather is terrible."

"They might be saying that to impress us, and show how hard they are. It will be colder and windier, but might not rain so much."

"We could write to Tom's brother and let him know we are coming. and stay at the inn where he works until we find somewhere else."

"When would we go?"

"We need to go back towards home and then another thirty miles or so," said Benjie, listening to the weather outside. "I think we should wait for the first fine day. It would be a miserable journey in weather like this."

"How long can we afford to stay?" asked Nancy.

"Quite a while if necessary," said Benjie. "Er, would you mind writing the letter?"

"No, of course not. But you could do it as well as I could, with all your education," she said.

"I never got any practice with pen and ink," he said, looking doubtfully at the quills and inkwell on the desk." I would hate to make a mess in this lovely room."

There was a knock on the door and the waiter brought their supper. Nancy had not felt hungry, but bread and cheese and pickles had never tasted so good. She was disappointed that there was no tea, but she was getting a taste for small beer.

***

It was a cold, bright, crisp, sunny morning when they started for Hilltop, two days later. Benjie and Nancy were both excited about their new life, and had lots of plans for a carting business and a little house of their own.

"I hope you are not catching a cold."

"Stop fussing, I am fine." said Benjie, sneezing.

"Charlie did a good job, getting your things over to us without anyone noticing. He mended your clothes as well. You will miss your little cousin," said Nancy.

"Very much," said Benjie, "and you will miss your family too."

"It will be very quiet without my sisters arguing," said Nancy, sadly.

"We will have to do something about that," said Benjie and proceeded to tickle her. There were giggles from Nancy, a fit of coughing from Benjie and a certain amount of confusion from the horse.

***

Towards the evening the weather started to get worse, the sky became grey instead of blue, and gradually became leaden. A few flakes of snow started to fall as they got nearer to their destination. Benjie and Nancy had brought some food with them, and had been planning to stop for a break, but in view of the weather they decided to press on before the snow became heavier.

Benjie was coughing more, and becoming weary so he even allowed Nancy to drive for a while, while he lay back under the cover. Towards the end, the snow was so heavy, and the road so treacherous, that he took up the reins again. Nancy was quite happy to let him drive, as the cart was less likely to overturn; they would be safe in the short term.

Nancy had put the distant future and the inquest out of her mind, as she worried whether Benjie had caught a chill. Could it be a serious chill? The cough did not worry her, although it sounded bad. She was more concerned by his tiredness, and the way he had given up the reins without a fight earlier on and was content to rest. The road was becoming impossible as they slowly plodded on; they were the last horse and cart into Hilltop before the town was cut off.

Joe was at the door looking for them when they finally arrived. Nancy got down very stiffly, glad to stretch her legs after the long ride. Benjie almost fell off the cart; Joe caught him before he hit the floor. He was very quiet and his face was white.

Benjie wanted to see to the horse and unpack the cart, but Joe insisted that they should both sit by the fire and have some hot, spiced wine. Benjie did not argue, which was not like him. It was lovely to rest in the warm and Joe was really pleased to have visitors from home and said that they could stay with him as long as they liked. Even so, Nancy worried whether it snowed a lot in winter, and would they have the strength to live and work in the highest settlement in England.

34 THE INQUEST

Tom sat in the courtroom, waiting for the Coroner to begin; he had attended quite a few inquests and always found it depressing. He felt that so many deaths could have been prevented, with a little care. Tom's job had some joy when patients got better but the Coroner heard everybody's bad news.

The Coroner read a copy of the report (again) and looked at everyone over the top of his spectacles. He looked weary.

"Every year my New Year is spoilt by having to preside over an inquest where the death could have been avoided," said the Coroner. "Is Timothy Hetherington in court?"

Everyone looked around; who was Timothy Hetherington?

"Yes," said Ox.

"Did you identify the body?"

"Yes, it is my brother, Frank Hetherington."

"Is William Jarvis in court?" asked the Coroner, after waiting for the recorder to catch up. The recorder looked as if his New Year had been spoilt as well.

"I'm here," said William.

"I have read your report. Please tell us in your own words how the unfortunate man died. Spare the medical detail, for ladies and those of us with weak stomachs."

"The main cause of death was multiple injuries; his chest was crushed by a cart wheel," said William. The recorder winced.

"Were there any other contributing factors?" asked the Coroner.

"A fall from a horse just before he went under the wheel," said William. "He did not break his neck, but may have broken his back. It was difficult to tell, because of the mess."

"Anything else?" asked the Coroner. The recorder was struggling to keep up, but looked very green about the gills.

"A blow sustained earlier in the evening, during a food fight at the Queen's Arms," said William. "Frank Hetherington was unconscious for some time and was probably concussed."

"Did anyone witness Frank receiving a blow to the head?" asked the Coroner.

Half the people said that they had seen a tankard hit Frank, but nobody remembered who had thrown it. There was a discussion of the evening, and the food fight in particular, and the Coroner had to call the court to order.

"Let us get on with this hearing," he said, "I want to get my dinner."

This was all too much for the recorder, who rushed out of the court with his hand over his mouth.

"The court will adjourn for thirty minutes," said the Coroner "Or however long it takes."

***

The court reconvened a little while later, when the recorder was a bit more composed.

"Were there any people present when you examined the body?" asked the Coroner, sneaking a look at the recorder who was intently studying some papers in front of him and gripping the edges tightly.

Tom, Ox and the carpenter all said that they were present and had nothing to add.

"Were there any witnesses to the death?" asked the Coroner.

"I saw it, but could not prevent it," said Tom.

"Tell us in your own words how it happened."

"Frank was chasing a cart driven by Benjie Armstrong and Nancy Graham. He came up behind them on Nancy's side, and tried to board the cart and stop them from continuing their journey to Gretna."

"Who did the horse and cart belong to?"

"Miss Graham."

"Continue," said the Coroner.

"Just as Frank let go of the reins to reach for the cart, the horse slipped on the ice. The horse righted itself, but Frank lost his balance and fell under the cart wheel."

"In your opinion, could they have avoided the cart running over him?"

"It all happened so quickly, there was no way the accident could have been avoided. A cart cannot be stopped instantly."

"Were there any other witnesses?" asked the Coroner.

"Benjie Armstrong and Nancy Graham," said Tom.

"Are they present in court?"

"No," said Richard.

"Do you know where they are?"

:d a letter from Gretna, saying that Mr. and Mrs. Armstrong were
, to go to Hilltop. I do not know if they went. Hilltop is cut off at the
.ent, with great big drifts of snow, and nobody can get in or out." said
.hard.

"Any more witnesses?" asked the Coroner.

"I didn't see the fall, but was on the scene shortly afterwards," said Richard.
"Dr. Harrison's version of events appears to be correct."

"It looks as if Frank was unlucky, falling from the horse and ending up
under the cart wheel," said the Coroner "I expect to record a verdict of
misadventure."

"Fair enough," said Ox.

"Just a minute," said Martha, "Frank did not fall accidentally, they
murdered him to steal my horse."

There was uproar in court as things suddenly became more interesting.

"Where is the horse now?" asked the Coroner.

"It never came back," said Martha. "They must have forced it to go to
Gretna with them because it would never have gone of its own free will.
Star is a very valuable horse."

Suppressed laughter went around the court as everyone imagined Star as a
valuable horse.

"Did Nancy and Benjie have Star with them when you saw them last?"
asked the Coroner.

"We tried to catch the horse for Mr. Armstrong, but he ran off and I did
not see in which direction, as it was dark," said Tom.

"Don't believe him, they are all in it together. They have hidden the horse
somewhere, because my horse would never run away. If he got loose he
would come home so that he could be cared for," said Martha.

"There was no sign of an extra horse when I arrived," said Richard.

"Don't believe him, he is Nancy's father. It is all a plot to rob a poor old
woman of her horse," said Martha.

"Are you doubting my word?" shouted Richard, moving towards Martha
who was snivelling into a grubby handkerchief.

The court became noisy again and the Coroner called for order.

"It looks as if I have to ask a few more questions before this case can be
closed. I need to talk to Mr. and Mrs. Armstrong, to find out exactly how
the man fell off the horse and confirm that the cart ran over him straight
away. I need to speak to witnesses at the Queen's Arms about the fight
earlier in the evening. It would be helpful to know why Frank was chasing
the couple in the cart. And I need to find out whether Mr. and Mrs.
Armstrong had an additional horse with them when they arrived at their
destination," said the Coroner. "Has anyone got anything else to say before
we adjourn"?

"I need to know the truth about my horse," said Martha. "And how poor

Frank died, of course."

"The court will adjourn," said the Coroner. "A date will be fixed when witnesses can travel from Hilltop. I have heard the medical and identification evidence, so the body can be released for burial."

35 THE WITNESS

The weather was cold and windy, but the thaw had started and Hilltop was no longer cut off from the rest of the world. Tom was going to arrange for Elizabeth to come home, as she was very keen to see her friends and family again.

The inquest was to be reopened the following afternoon, and Benjie and Nancy would be travelling back at the same time. Ideally Elizabeth and her belongings would travel on the cart and Tom would ride alongside on Thunderbolt.

Tom was looking forward to bringing Elizabeth home; it was wonderful that she was well again, even if she had to be careful. He had been so worried when she was showing all the early signs of consumption, but a few months at Hilltop had made all the difference. If Elizabeth did not work in the mill, she would probably stay healthy.

Tom wondered if his family would be impressed, and rather doubted it. He had respect from the townspeople, they believed in him and trusted him but he felt sure that his own family just saw him as a young lad, and not as a qualified doctor.

Tom wondered what would happen at the inquest. If they questioned Nancy on how Frank fell off the cart, would Benjie claim to have run over the man on purpose? It didn't bear thinking about. Surely the coroner would see that Benjie couldn't possible have stopped in time. Wouldn't he?

***

Tom was very surprised to see Nancy in the inn yard, waiting for him. She seemed to be wearing several shawls and sheltering against the wind.

"I am really worried about Benjie, he is not well at all," said Nancy.

"What is the problem?" asked Tom.

"He caught a nasty chill on the day we came here in all that snow. He was getting better when we were snowbound indoors, but now he insists on driving the cart all day and is making himself worse. You talk to him, he won't listen to me," said Nancy. This was not the sort of thing that Tom expected Nancy to say; perhaps Benjie was not as biddable as she had hoped.

Tom saw Benjie driving the cart towards them; he had a young lad with him. Tom was saddened by the change in Benjie since he saw him last; he was coughing and looked very pale and tired.

"Hello Tom," said Benjie. "This is Alice's cousin, Nipper. He got his name because he is always nipping off school to hang around the stables. He has been helping me load and unload."

Another fit of coughing followed; Benjie got down and held on to the cart to steady himself.

"Don't worry, I will see to the horse and cart," said Nipper.

"Shouldn't you be at school this afternoon?" asked Benjie. "I can manage." But Nipper and the cart had gone.

"You don't look well at all, Benjie," said Tom. "I think I had better have a look at you. You are still my patient, you know."

"I'm fine," said Benjie, still protesting as Tom led him indoors.

"We have been managing fine in Hilltop. There is plenty of carting work when we are not snowbound, things to take between the little villages that make up the town. Elizabeth has been running a little dame school when we were cut off, so the children don't miss their lessons. Nancy has been helping her," said Benjie.

Tom smiled to himself at the idea of Nancy as Elizabeth's helper.

"Can you just stop talking for a minute while I listen to your chest?" asked Tom. "Hmm. As I thought. Very worrying. You have a chest fever and must go to bed immediately. Keep warm and have plenty to drink. I will give you something for the cough."

"I'm fine, honestly, just a bit of a cough," said Benjie.

"You have been overdoing things, you must look after yourself better. Especially now you are a married man with responsibilities. Think about how poor Nancy would feel if anything happened to you," said Tom.

"Maybe I do feel a bit tired but I am sure I will be fine after a good night's rest; I need to drive the cart tomorrow," said Benjie. Tom let that pass, but was quite sure that he would not let Benjie go anywhere near the cart in the morning.

***

"You look as if you could use another drink. I have some rather good ale that I would like you to try," said Joe.

The customers had gone; it was late. Nancy was fussing over Benjie, and Alice had gone to bed, after telling Joe that he shouldn't sit up too long.

"Your words are music to my ears, I need to get rid of some of the stiffness after the ride here," said Tom. "Mmm, this is rather good."

"Have some more, there is plenty," said Joe, as he topped up Tom's tankard. "It is a long ride; life would be much easier if young Robert built one of his railways for us."

"To hear him talk, you would think he was building the railways all by himself. He is very proud of his railways and won't hear a word against them."

"How are Robert and Bridget? I haven't seen Robert for ages, and I have not met Bridget yet."

"They're fine. They have a baby son; they are naming him after father. They have asked me to be godfather."

"That reminds me, Alice said I had to ask you to be Sarah's godfather. We will have the christening when the weather gets better."

"I would be happy to. My services are in demand."

"It will be confusing for you, all these babies named after our parents," said Joe, pouring more ale. "Er… I may be speaking out of turn, but wasn't mother expecting you to marry Nancy?"

"She was," said Tom. "She kept going on about it, and I am ashamed to say that I avoided mother and father for a while. I found it much more comfortable to live at the surgery."

"Who looks after you?"

"We manage, and young Charlie has learnt to cook a bit. There is a woman who comes in and cleans and takes the washing, but she knows her place. Some of our patients feel sorry for us and invite us to dinner. It suited me rather well, and I never went back home."

"And Nancy?"

"I am not sure, we just got cold feet. I think she finds me a bit stubborn," said Tom "Lovely girl though, just a bit…"

"I noticed," said Joe with a smile. "Have some more ale, we need to test it and make sure it is all right for the customers."

"Nancy and Benjie are well suited. But last time I saw Nancy, she looked different, and I wondered what would have happened if…" Tom stopped, gave a sigh and had a long drink.

"I am sure it is for the best."

"Nancy is the love of my life," said Tom, "I just couldn't live with her."

"Not many could."

"I think I am getting a bit maudlin in my cups," said Tom, as he felt his eyes water a little.

"Never," said Joe. "But if you can't do it here, where can you? Certainly not at the Queen's Arms at home."

"Arthur means well, but he can't keep secrets," said Tom. "And I am a doctor, I have to look as if I know what I am doing."

"You are an excellent doctor," said Joe. "You have done wonders for Elizabeth, sending her to us for a change of air."

"Now I'm really getting maudlin," said Tom. "Is there any more ale?"

"We might as well finish this jug, now we have started it," said Joe. It was a very large jug, three quarters full.

"I must visit more often."

"When you are married with a family of your own, you will not have time," said Joe.

"I will never marry. Not now."

"Surely you will."

"Never," said Tom, with a sigh. "To be honest, I can't be doing with a woman telling me what to do."

"I see what you mean," said Joe. "But in families there is often one brother or sister who stays single, and keeps tabs on all the others. Helps them out. There are a lot of us; me, Robert, George, Elizabeth, Mary Ann and all those godchildren! You have a family already."

"I am married to my work, and my apprentice keeps everybody guessing. You wouldn't believe what he did at the quoits match."

Sometime later, when the jug was empty, Tom got up from his chair and slithered onto the floor.

"I must be stiffer than I thought," said Tom.

"Of course you are," said Joe, a little unsteady on his feet as helped Tom up the stairs.

As they ascended, swaying and laughing, Tom realized that he felt better than he had for ages.

***

Tom didn't feel quite so good the next morning, as everyone was very noisy. There was a lot of unnecessary clattering and banging as Elizabeth's luggage was loaded on to the cart. And surely Nipper and Alice could talk to each other more quietly. And there was an argument somewhere that was getting louder all the time.

"I need to get dressed! Give me my clothes this minute!" shouted Benjie.

"You are not well enough to get up. Tell him, Tom!" wailed Nancy, as they burst into the room where Tom was having a very strong cup of tea. He didn't fancy anything to eat for breakfast, and the smell of bacon was making him heave.

"Benjie, I said you had to rest. You are not well enough to get up," said Tom.

"Told you," said Nancy, stridently, and Tom shuddered.

"I need to drive the cart, I promised to take Elizabeth home," said Benjie. "What will my customers think if I lie in bed all day and don't do my job?"

"Nipper will load the cart and I can drive," said Nancy, "the work will still get done."

"It is too far for you," said Benjie "I can't possibly allow it."

"I can help if necessary," said Tom "If you go today and the weather turns bad, you will be coming back in one of the carpenter's wooden boxes."

"Please do as he says," pleaded Nancy, bursting into tears.

"What about coming back," asked Benjie "You will be on your own, in the dark. I can't let you."

"I will be coming back," said Tom. "I have a patient to visit, and I had hoped to rest Thunderbolt today."

"Is there something the matter with Thunderbolt?" asked Benjie. "I will just go and see..."

"Back to bed!" shouted Tom. It was not Thunderbolt that needed rest from the previous day's ride.

"Do I have to tie you to that bed?" asked Nancy.

"Ooh, yes miss," said Benjie.

"Please go and rest!" cajoled Nancy. Tom had never heard her do that before.

***

They set off earlier rather than later, before Benjie changed his mind. Elizabeth was very excited to go home, and chattered for most of the journey but Tom and Nancy were rather quiet as they both felt a bit queasy.

36 THE VERDICT

Nancy found that the queasiness wore off by mid-morning, which gave her one less thing to worry about. She found Elizabeth's chatter rather wearing; Nancy could have done without all the questions about the school while she was trying to concentrate on her driving. Nancy had only driven short distances before, and she did not know the route very well. She had already learnt the hard way that it was very difficult to persuade the horse to turn and go in the opposite direction; it involved all three of them getting out and pushing, and providing bribes. Nancy concentrated on getting things right first time, if only to avoid seeing a look of amusement on Tom's face.

The preoccupation with the journey meant that she was not thinking about the inquest that afternoon, and what questions she would be asked. At least Benjie would not be there to jump in with a confession if the questions got too near the mark. She tried not to think about what would happen if Benjie took a time to recover, or did not recover at all.

Unloading Elizabeth and her belongings took longer than expected, as Sarah Harrison had parcels to take back for Joe and his family; these parcels were not to hand and Nancy felt that they should have thought ahead. At least they did not foresee that Nancy might not be going back. She might be imprisoned in the 'Jug' with the horse and cart stranded in Arthur's stables.

***

There had been delays to their journey all morning, so they had to turn down Sarah's offer of dinner and go straight into the court. They were the last people to arrive, and Nancy felt that everyone was looking at them as they went in. What was Hamish in court for? It had nothing to do with him! But the Coroner called him to the stand first and asked him whether Mr. and Mrs. Armstrong had arrived with more than one horse. Hamish testified that they had only one horse, a piebald one pulling the cart. Once he had solemnly sworn on the Bible that this was so, the Coroner told him that he was free to leave the court.

Why bring Hamish all this way, just to ask him about the horse?

"I have letters here from two reputable citizens at Hilltop, to say that Mr. and Mrs. Armstrong arrived with one horse, and a chestnut horse with a white blaze has not been seen anywhere in the area," said the Coroner. He handed the letters to the recorder.

Nancy was indignant when she realized what had been implied. She was about to say so, when a look from her father changed her mind. The idea of it! As if they had wanted to steal that bad-tempered, ill-favoured horse! But then she remembered that Benjie was rather fond of Star for some reason.

Arthur was called next, to give evidence about the fight in the earlier part of the evening.

"How did the fight start?" asked the Coroner. "Remember that you are under oath."

"There was an argument between Martha Armstrong's gang and the quarry workers, over a recent death. Frank said that the quarrymen did not look after their workers properly. The quarrymen said that the gang should not have sent Caleb to the quarry because he was too young," said Arthur.

"The quarrymen were quite correct," said the Coroner. "Who threw the first missile?"

"Frank did," said Arthur. "He threw a stool, and then everybody started throwing things; it started a bit earlier than usual this year."

"Are you telling me that this happens every year, and is encouraged?"

"They look forward to it all year. We sell lots of ale and it doesn't take long to clear up afterwards. I usually make a bit of a protest, to make it more fun for them."

"And what happened to Frank during the fight?"

"He was hit by a tankard and knocked out. I can't remember who threw it, I think it was one of the gang, they were aiming for someone else."

"And what happened to Frank after that?"

"We would have taken him home, but the wheelbarrow was already in use. So Frank had to wait; we mainly forgot about him and had our food, or what was left of it."

"So you just left an injured man on the floor?"

"He was a bit big to lift. And we thought he might bear a grudge, so we thought it best to wait until his brother was there to help, and then he got woken up."

"How did that happen?"

"A few people fell on him during Auld Lang Syne, I think they were a bit merry."

"So he could have sustained further injuries at that stage" said the Coroner, with a sigh. "It gets worse. What happened next?"

"He wasn't pleased and started arguing again. And then Martha Armstrong came in, as she does, once her laudanum has worn off," said Arthur.

"What happened then?"

"We had worked out that young Benjie Armstrong had eloped with Nancy Graham. So Mrs. Martha Armstrong told Frank to follow them and fetch him back. And Dr. Jarvis advised against it because Frank had hit his head, but he went anyway," said Arthur.

"That will be all for now," said the Coroner. "Is Mr. Benjamin Armstrong in court?"

"No, he is dangerously ill, with a high fever. I considered that he would not survive the journey if he attended the inquest," said Tom.

Nancy was shocked; she hadn't realised how ill Benjie was. Was Tom saying that it would kill him to make the journey? That meant he might die anyway? Nancy had not heard it spelt out quite like that, and tried to compose herself before she gave evidence.

"That is very unfortunate, Dr. Harrison. If this business is not resolved today, we may have to adjourn again. When is he likely to be available?" asked the Coroner.

"I can't say," said Tom, "maybe not at all. His constitution is weak. He was another under age quarry worker."

"Living at the barracks, surely, after my recommendation?" said the Coroner, looking around the court.

"No, we wanted him to, but he wasn't allowed," answered the quarry foreman. "Mrs. Martha Armstrong said it cost her too much for her men to live in our barracks."

"I see. Nothing ever gets done!" said the Coroner with a sigh. "Is Mrs. Benjamin Armstrong in court?"

Nancy's reply was almost inaudible, and her hand shook as she took the oath. She felt as if she was miles away and that none of this was happening. All she could think about was Benjie, and how ill he was. It was all her fault, if she hadn't insisted on him running off to Gretna, he would never have caught that chill.

"I understand that you ran off to Gretna to be married. Why was that? You left your father to look after two children, and you left the school with no teacher for your class," said the Coroner, sternly.

"Benjie's grandmother would not give permission for him to marry as he was under age. She said she needed his wages until he was of age."

"And you couldn't wait?"

"We would have, only after young Caleb died, I thought Benjie would be next," said Nancy, with a wobble in her voice. "Only now he will die anyway and it was all for nothing."

"Can you tell me what happened?" said the Coroner in a kinder voice.

"My family and I got the horse and cart ready and Benjie met me at the crossroads. We were all right until we got nearly into Carlisle and we saw Frank riding along the road after us."

"What happened next?"

"Frank caught up, and tried to push us into the ditch and overturn the cart," said Nancy, "and then he tried to climb up onto the cart behind me. I was so frightened. I thought he was going to kill us and I didn't know what to do!"

"And what did you do?" asked the Coroner. Tom held his breath.

"I was saying my prayers, waiting for the end, when he fell off his horse under the wheel," said Nancy with a sob.

"That is consistent with Dr. Harrison's account, and also with the injuries," said the Coroner. "I have to ask you, what happened to his horse?"

"We tried to catch it, but it ran away. It didn't seem important, and we had to steady our own horse or we would have been stranded. It all happened in such a rush," said Nancy.

"That will be all for now," said the Coroner. "Dr. Tom Harrison?"

Tom was surprised that he had been called again, but took the oath as directed.

"Why did you set off after Mr. Hetherington?" asked the Coroner.

"Mr. Graham and I were anxious that nobody should come to any harm, so we set off as soon as we could. Frank was very large and known to be violent. My horse was faster than Mr. Graham's and I arrived just before he did," said Tom.

"Very commendable," said the Coroner, "what did you see as the main danger?"

"Frank was a known bully and we thought that he might injure or kill the young couple. I was helping a father protect his daughter," said Tom, "and Frank was in danger himself, riding out on icy roads at night, so soon after that blow on the head."

There were murmurs of agreement in court. After Richard's evidence, the Coroner asked for Mrs. Martha Armstrong.

Martha had been waiting impatiently for her turn all afternoon.

"All this happened because Benjie wanted to run off with some brazen hussy instead of staying with his legal guardian."

"Will you please take the oath," said the Coroner.

"You couldn't expect him to live a live a life of luxury in the barracks at those prices, and leave his poor old grandmother to starve."

The recorder handed her the Bible.

"Frank was only going to fetch my property back, Benjie should have come back with him instead of driving off," said Martha. "What's this for?"

"I want you to swear an oath that you will tell the truth," said the Coroner. "Repeat the words after the recorder."

"Don't you believe me?"

"You still have to swear the oath," said the Coroner. It had been a long day. "I want to ask you why you didn't take care of Benjamin. I want to ask you why you let Frank bully your workers. I want to ask you why you sent Frank out after Benjamin against medical advice."

"I have never sworn an oath in my life and I don't intend to start now," said Martha indignantly.

"Then you can't give evidence," said the Coroner wearily as he prepared to sum up.

"I still haven't got my horse back," muttered Martha as she went back to her place.

"There is no evidence of theft, and no motive for an unlawful killing. I am going to record an open verdict; any or all of the injuries may have caused the death, it is difficult to say. Nobody is directly responsible for the death, but that does not mean that you are all blameless.

"The people at the New Year party ignored an injured man lying on the floor. The innkeepers and druggists encourage the sale of ale and laudanum that befuddle the wits and interfere with good judgement. The young couple ran off without a thought for their responsibilities, though they may be punished by a higher authority than me," said the Coroner.

"Serves them right," said Martha.

"I will ignore that interruption," said the Coroner. "Above all, the unfortunate man brought his death on himself because of his rash actions. The quarry owners must make sure that their workers are looked after, and the barracks affordable. Gangmasters must look after their workers and not allow them to be overworked and bullied. This is the third recent death out of this particular gang and there may soon be a fourth. Everybody seems to be keen on making a few extra pennies and putting their own interests ahead of those of their neighbours. Greed, carelessness, and negligence cause most of these deaths that could have been prevented. I hope you have all learnt a lesson, but I don't suppose you have."

37 THE CRISIS

Nancy spent the night with her family, they were very glad to see her. She would have preferred to go straight back to Benjie, but it was too late in the day to set out. She felt a little guilty about abandoning her family and her school class.

"Don't worry about us, we will manage. Not as well as if you were looking after us," Richard said hastily," but it will do us good to learn to fend for ourselves."

"And the school?" Nancy asked.

"They have depended on you for far too long," said Richard, "they will have to get another teacher or pupil teacher. Susan says that there were so many new children in the infant class that some of the older girls have had to help out."

"I would never have become headmistress if I had stayed. Women run dame schools, but they always have a headmaster for a proper school."

"You would never have got any further as a teacher, but if you are prepared to work you could make a real success of the carting business. Many carters get into a muddle because nobody keeps track of the work or the money."

Nancy resolved that sort of thing would never happen to them, but she was worried what would happen if Benjie did not get better quickly. She tried not to think what would happen if he did not get better at all.

"How can I manage when Benjie is ill? I can't drive the cart all day."

"How did you get here then?"

"Oh!" she said. "But what about loading and unloading?"

"Charge less if your customers load and unload their own goods. Have you any help?"

"Alice's cousin, Nipper, helps Benjie with the horse; he is very keen but he should be at school."

"Train Nipper up to help you, pay him a boy's wage or give him schooling. Take things one day at a time," said Richard.

Nancy drew some comfort from her family, but still worried whether Benjie would survive the illness. When she finally fell asleep, she dreamt that the Coroner had convicted her of murder, and Benjie's death would be her punishment.

Early next morning, Tom and Nancy set off for Hilltop; they were both thinking of the Coroner's words the day before. Nancy felt that the open verdict left a lot of doubt about Frank's death, and she still felt responsible. And why was Tom returning to Hilltop? He did not usually visit people in Westmorland; he must be really worried about his patient.

"Are you feeling all right?" asked Tom.

"Not really," she said, "I didn't sleep much."

"Neither did I. I kept thinking about what the Coroner said."

"I feel so guilty. Benjie's illness is my punishment. But he should not be punished, he never did anything wrong."

"The Coroner seemed to think that the whole town was guilty. There were things I hadn't thought were wrong. I must ask Dr. Jarvis about it all next time I see him. Shall I drive for a bit, give you a rest?"

"I feel a bit better when I am concentrating on the road. Maybe you could drive for a bit later when my sickness wears off."

"Do you feel sick every morning?"

"I think it is the movement of the cart. I need to get used to it."

"It might not be the cart. Was your mother very sick before the twins were born?"

"Yes, she was, I hadn't thought of that," she said, trying to take in this new idea. Nipper could definitely do the early morning work, especially taking smelly pigs to market.

***

Alice met Tom and Nancy when they got back, and they could tell from her face that she did not have good news for them.

"Benjie seems to be getting worse," she said, "he tried to get up this morning and collapsed. We put him back to bed and he didn't even argue."

Tom grabbed his bag and rushed indoors, leaving Nancy to deal with the horse and cart. When she finally saw Benjie, he sank back on his pillows, exhausted after a fit of coughing. He was hot to the touch, and very quiet.

"Benjie! Are you all right?" she asked, although she knew the answer.

"My head hurts," he said, "and I feel so tired I can hardly stand but Dr. Tom will make me better."

"You need rest, plenty to drink. Have you been taking your cough medicine?" asked Tom.

"It tastes horrible," said Benjie, with a flicker of his old smile. "What was the verdict?"

"Open verdict. The Coroner couldn't work out whether it was the accident or injuries from the fight at the ale house," said Tom.

"Did he blame us?"

"He blamed Frank mainly, and the whole town for letting it happen. The Coroner tries to keep everybody safe, but if we did as he said we would never get any work done or have any fun. You don't need to worry about Frank. Ox certainly doesn't blame you."

"Is he still working at the quarry?"

"Yes, but he left the gang and is living in the barracks. He is helping the new labourers as best he can."

"And my grandmother?"

"Still fretting about her horse."

"Poor old Star, I wonder where he got to?" said Benjie, and started to cough again.

"I expect he is having a better time than we are," said Tom, "now try and get some rest. You will be up and about in a few days."

***

Benjie was not up and about in a few days as hoped; he slept more, and grew weaker as time wore on. Nancy realised that Tom had been worried about him and had come back to Hilltop just to help Benjie. When Tom had told the Coroner that Benjie's life would be in danger if he travelled, it was nearer to the truth than she thought.

It was heart breaking to sit with Benjie. He was sleeping fitfully a lot of the time; he was obviously in pain when he woke. Tom sat with Benjie most of the time; Joe, Alice and Nancy took a turn when the demands of the inn, children and carting business allowed.

Benjie slept more and more; they found it difficult to wake him. He talked constantly in his sleep – his early years with his parents, the death of his mother, his grandmother's place, the death of his father, work in the gang. They all found it heart breaking to listen to. Finally, there was the death of young Caleb, and Nancy found it so hard to bear. He had such a hard life, and now it was over.

"Can't you cure him?" asked Nancy, but she was afraid that she knew the answer.

"I can ease the symptoms, and make him feel better. But he must fight the disease himself," said Tom with a sob. He knew he sounded unprofessional but it was the first time one of his friends was dying and he felt so helpless. Benjie was very young; it was so unfair.

"Can you give him something to ease the pain?" asked Nancy.

"I give laudanum to the dying, but it slows the breathing. Benjie still has a fighting chance, I don't want to give in just yet," said Tom. But he knew it might not be long before he had to.

170

"What can we do?" asked Nancy.

"Watch, wait and pray," said Tom. Words he had said before, but this time they applied to Tom as well as Nancy.

Alice came in to say that Benjie had fallen into a deep sleep, and she couldn't wake him so Tom and Nancy went back into the sickroom.

"What do I do now?" asked Nancy.

"Sit with him. He may be having a crisis before he gets better or it could be the end. He would want you to be with him. Talk to him, he may hear you even if he doesn't answer. Read to him, it might just stop him slipping away. Tell him about future plans, to give him something to look forward to. Have you told him about the baby?" asked Tom.

"But I am not sure if..." said Nancy.

"Tell him anyway. Anything to keep him with us," said Tom.

All that night Nancy held Benjie's hand and talked to him. She told him that they would need to look for a house for themselves and the baby. She told him that the carting was going well. She read to him as best she could by the light of the flickering candle.

Just before dawn, Benjie seemed less restless, just cold and pale. Nancy knew it was the end, but she made one last effort.

"Don't go to sleep, we need you. I am expecting twins in the autumn and they need a father," said Nancy.

Benjie opened his eyes, looked at her and smiled. His breathing seemed much quieter as he closed his eyes again. It was Nancy who held her breath.

38 THE HOMECOMING

The February sun shone bleakly as Tom set off for home. He still felt dazed and tired: couldn't quite take in the fact that Benjie was recovering. Perhaps his hard life as a youngster had made him stronger, or Nancy's love and devotion had pulled him through. It certainly wasn't Tom's skill; there was no cure for the fever and the doctor could not fight the battle for the patient.

Tom was now riding away from Nancy, and towards his responsibilities. Would he marry and settle down? Could he think of anyone else after Nancy? What would have happened if…?

***

"You look tired," said William as Tom came in to the shop, "you could have stayed longer and rested. Charlie and I were managing so well; I have just given him an afternoon off."

"Once Benjie was out of danger I didn't need to stay any longer," said Tom. "But it was touch and go at one time."

"So I gathered from your letter," said William, "but it is fairly quiet here. Everyone's being careful; they must have listened to that Coroner and there have been no fights for days."

"I couldn't understand what he meant about laudanum, I meant to ask you."

"That's a difficult one," said William with a sigh. "Laudanum is made from opium poppies. It can ease a man's pain or his passing and it can make life seem bearable when it isn't."

"Is that so bad?"

"People get to depend on it and they take it regularly to blot out the world. Everybody knows about Dr. Godfrey's Cordial; they even give it to babies to keep them quiet."

"Should we stop selling it?" asked Tom, "or restrict it for medical use?"

"We make a lot of money from it," said William, "and if we didn't sell it someone else would."

"But if it's harmful?"

"Life can be so hard, laudanum might be a man's only pleasure," said William. "And life is usually very short, we can't grudge it. But if someone takes it for a long time, it becomes less effective and they have to take more and more until they are spending most of their money on it."

"Like Martha Armstrong?" asked Tom.

"When the boys first left home, and she was widowed, she discovered how to make the pain go away; our predecessor helped her. She made a living as best she could but had to make more and more money to keep herself in laudanum. But for every person like her there are hundreds like Wiggy who can be helped to a pain-free death." said William, "There is no easy answer."

They watched the children playing kiss chase outside. Charlie was chasing Susan; she was just putting up enough of a fight so she didn't appear too eager. Mary Ann was enjoying herself, but Elizabeth and Adam considered themselves too old to join in, and stood talking to each other. Tom had always thought that football was much more fun than kiss chase when he was at school. "You never married, William, did you?" asked Tom, "Was there anyone?"

"Once," said William. "But I couldn't bear the thought of losing her, especially through childbirth. I couldn't put her through that. And then work got in the way."

"Did you regret not marrying?" asked Tom.

"Not really," said William. "I never had children of my own but you and Charlie kept me busy."

Tom grinned at the thought of Charlie's recent escapades, and his own previous ones.

"How about you?" asked William, "Will you marry and settle down?"

"Nobody could hold a candle to Nancy," said Tom. "Not anywhere near."

"Would you have married her if Benjie had not survived?" asked William.

"I don't think I would," said Tom. "I will never know. I think I'll go and see my parents this evening."

"About time," said William.

***

"How was school today, Elizabeth?" asked Sarah. "It seems funny to be asking you that again after all this time."

"It's getting better," said Elizabeth, "I teach the youngest children, the others are divided between Mr. Watson, Mrs. Hull, and Adam. He is doing ever so well; he has a class of his own and he has only been teaching for a

173

short while."

"So have you," said Mary Ann, "and your class is the most difficult. Miss Graham's old class wouldn't say boo to a goose, and Adam has most of those."

"Adam is doing really well; Mr. Watson is showing him lots of paperwork. He says he might be headmaster one day," said Elizabeth.

"And are your children all right, or still crying for their mothers?" asked Tom.

"Some of them are crying for Mrs. Hull; they feel that she has gone and left them and that their mothers don't want them either. Adam says…" said Elizabeth.

"Susan, Sally and I go in and help sometimes if they get too noisy. We have a little sing and everybody feels better," said Mary Ann.

"Do you like teaching?" asked Tom.

"Not really, but Susan does. I would like to be a dressmaker like you, Jeannie," said Mary Ann. "Making hats would be even better."

"It is a long apprenticeship and hard work," said Jeannie.

"I am not sure about another apprenticeship in the family," said Sarah.

"Tom was allowed to be an apprentice, mother. Why can't I?" whined Mary Ann.

"It's good to have a trade in these uncertain times," said John. "If the apprenticeship is not too expensive."

"There was talk about short time at the mill," said George.

"A dressmaker's apprentice has no money for the first two years," said Jeannie, "but learns a skill."

"We will see," said Sarah.

"Please," pleaded Mary Ann.

"It is good to be all together again," said Sarah, "we only seem to get together for weddings."

"I have had enough of those for a while. Yours was all right, George, but the others had one or two problems," said Tom.

"I hope you girls never do what Miss Graham did!" said Sarah.

"No, mother," they said, although they thought it might be romantic.

"Or what Bridget did," said John.

"Certainly not, father," they said, although they thought it might be fun.

"I had hoped that you would be next to be married, Tom," said Sarah.

"I have no plans to marry," said Tom.

"Not at the moment, but maybe after a while," said Sarah.

"Not at all, ever." said Tom. He felt better now he had said it.

"You can't really want to live in that messy surgery. You need a wife or mother looking after you, making sure your clothes are clean and mended, your meals on time and you don't spend too much time in the ale house or out gallivanting. That is why Nancy would have been so good for you. But you let her slip away and then look what happened," said Sarah.

"I find the surgery strangely restful," said Tom. "Leave us bachelors alone." John and George smiled to themselves.

"Perhaps I should come over sometimes and make sure that you are all right. A woman's touch, perhaps," said Sarah.

"No need for that, mother," said Tom, sharply.

"I only meant it for your own good," said Sarah.

"I know, but I am happy as I am. Old Tom Sawbones, disreputable bachelor. If he isn't at the surgery, try the ale house. Anyway, one of your brood should stay single. Keep the family in touch with each other. Look after the old folk and keep them out of the poorhouse, that sort of thing." said Tom.

"The very idea of the poorhouse!" said Sarah.

"It could happen to anyone," said John.

"Caleb's mother went in last week," said Mary Ann.

"If someone has no means of support, and no family to help…" said John.

"Could it happen to people like us?" asked Sarah.

"The town has always been prosperous in the past, but times are changing. It depends on the mill," said John.

"I had expected one of the girls to stay single and look after us," said Sarah.

"No need to hold them back," said Tom. Elizabeth blushed.

"I think Elizabeth has someone in mind, already," said Mary Ann.

"How can you look after us, Tom? You can't clean, cook or sew," said Sarah.

"It doesn't take much to keep a place tidy," said Tom. Mary Ann thought of the surgery and opened her eyes wide in surprise.

"And I can bring pies from the shop," said Tom.

"I suppose," said Sarah.

"And I can sew after a fashion," said Tom, "but I find it easier to sew up people rather than clothes."

Sarah and Jeannie shuddered, but the others were amused.

"Anyway, I must go back to that untidy surgery. Dr. Jarvis and I will smoke a smelly pipe, and wander over to the ale house. We don't have the same home comforts as you married men, so we have to get our amusement where we can," said Tom. George and John looked rather envious.

39 THE EPILOGUE

Outside their window Nancy and Benjie could hear the rain and the howling of the wind; the weather seemed to turn 'backendish' sooner at Hilltop than it did at home. Their terrace house was warm and cosy, with shelter for their horse and cart in the yard. Nancy thought that her house was just as nice as her friend Jeannie's; it was such a shame about the weather.

"You are clever, Nancy, how did you know you were expecting twins?" asked Benjie, as he looked into the cradle again.

"I felt so sick, I was sure that it was more than one baby," said Nancy. "My mother was the same."

"At least we will be able to tell the boys apart. The one on the right is much bigger."

"Yes he takes after my side of the family, built like a proper little blacksmith," said Nancy with a smile, "and the other one looks more like you."

"Yes, he reminds me of Charlie when he was a baby. He has the family nose; he will grow into that face. Notice that he is making most of the noise."

"Little Benjamin, after your father; and Richard after mine. I wonder what will become of them."

"They will learn trades," said Benjie," no poorhouse or farm labour gangs for them. Nothing but the best."

"But what happens if we don't see them grow up," said Nancy with tears in her eyes.

"We choose godfathers who will see them right. The big twin will be Richard William or Dickon."

"Dr. Jarvis would be a good choice of godfather."

"And the smaller twin will be named Benjamin Thomas, or Tommy."

"If you think Tom can handle the responsibility. What was that knock at the door earlier on?" Even though Nancy was resting in bed after the birth, nothing in their little house got past her.

"Joe brought a letter over from the inn." Benjie looked at the unopened letter. "I never get letters; it looks important. Here, you read it."

"You read it, you don't want to waste all those lessons," said Nancy. They both smiled as they remembered the lessons, it seemed such a long time ago.

"I have to go to a hearing with some governors," said Benjie, "I thought that business about Frank was all over. Could they have found out something and reopened the inquest? Or could there be a murder trial?"

"Here, let me have a look," said Nancy. "It is from the poorhouse governors. They say that one of your relatives has applied to be an inmate, but they want to see if any of the family can provide for them."

"It must be Charlie, perhaps he has done something dreadful and Tom is sending him back," said Benjie.

"Perhaps the practice has failed and they have no choice," said Nancy, "It wouldn't surprise me. I don't see how they can ever find anything in that shop. Perhaps George would be better as a godfather."

"I must fetch Charlie to live with us," said Benjie.

"Of course," said Nancy. "But it might not be him, it could be a more distant relative. Don't be bringing back half the town."

Benjie had to tear himself away from Nancy and the babies and get the horse and cart ready for his journey.

***

Benjie arrived to find the shop the same as usual, and Charlie did not seem to be in any sort of disgrace.

"How's Nancy?" asked William.

"Nancy and the twins are fine," said Benjie, and went on at length about how wonderful his family were.

"What brings you here?" asked Tom, "Not that we aren't pleased to see you."

"I got a letter from the poorhouse governors," said Benjie, "they say that a relative has applied to be an inmate. I thought it was you, and brought the cart to take you back with me."

"I have a letter like yours," said Charlie. "Our grandmother is about to go into the poorhouse."

"How did that happen?" asked Benjie.

"She was all right for the first couple of months, although she hadn't many workers left, and no horse, but she came into the shop as usual. Then her workers started hiring themselves out at the start of the season, until she had no one left. She couldn't get a job anywhere, even at the mill. She sold the cart, which kept her going for a bit. Eventually she couldn't pay her rent, and she is to be evicted," said Tom.

"We are not selling as much laudanum these days," said William, "so we have to do more real work."

"They are asking if we can support her," said Charlie, "but I am only a boy apprentice with no money and no home of my own."

"Normally it would be my duty," said Benjie, "but I can't afford to, I have my own family to think about. Anyway, I don't live in the parish."

***

"We are here today to see if this woman is destitute, or if her friends and family can support her. Is Timothy Hetherington here?" asked the governor.

"Yes," answered Ox.

"I understand that you lodged with Mrs. Armstrong for several years. Is it possible for you to lodge with her again so that she can pay her rent?" asked the governor. He really didn't want this difficult old woman causing trouble in his poorhouse.

"No," said Ox, "I work in a quarry some miles away, and live in the barracks."

"It's near enough to walk to work every morning, you lazy lump," said Martha.

"Could you offer her a home there?" asked the governor, hopefully.

Ox looked at the quarry foreman, who shook his head.

"No", said Ox, "sorry."

"That will be all, Mr. Hetherington, you may leave. Mrs. Armstrong, I understand that you ran a farm labour gang for many years. Didn't you save any money to carry you over hard times?" asked the governor, in the hope that she would remember about a sum of money stashed away somewhere.

"It was very difficult to make ends meet; I had to pay the men a good wage," said Martha. A wave of laughter went around the court.

"I had to provide good food for my workers. It was expensive, and so was the ale," said Martha. Benjie and Ox tried to hide a smile, but Arthur looked uncomfortable.

"The prices they charged for tobacco and laudanum! So they could send good for nothing young doctors gallivanting off to foreign parts!" said Martha. Now it was William and Tom's turn to look uncomfortable.

"Then my workers all went off and deserted me," said Martha. But Ox had already gone.

"I must ask the applicant's grandsons if they can help, although I understand that they are both under age," said the governor.

"My grandsons won't desert me. Both are old enough to work and do their duty," said Martha.

"I'm an apprentice; my indentures say that I cannot earn money yet. I have no home of my own, and must lodge with my masters," said Charlie, trying to look younger than he was. He was not too convincing because his voice was getting deeper.

"You ungrateful boy! I offered you a home! You must leave your apprenticeship and get a proper job and do your duty by your family," said Martha.

"Sorry, I cannot break my indentures," said Charlie, and stepped back to join William and Tom, where he felt safer.

"Mr. Benjamin Armstrong, are you in a position to support your relative?" asked the governor.

"No, I have recently married and set up home. I have a wife and two small babies," said Benjie, "I cannot contribute to her rent."

"I have given you a home for years, since your good for nothing parents died. Kept you, fed you, clothed you and asked for nothing in return," said Martha.

"I live outside the parish," said Benjie.

"Perhaps the applicant could make her home with you," said the governor, hopefully.

"Give a home to your poor old grandmother, spare your family the shame of the poorhouse," said Martha as she flourished her handkerchief.

Benjie looked as if he was wavering.

"Mr. Armstrong has been very ill this year. As his doctor I would not advise him to take his grandmother into his home. For health reasons," said Tom.

"If it's difficult to make ends meet, I could look after your babies while your wife works," wheedled Martha.

"I will not have that woman anywhere near my children!" said Benjie. His face was stern, an image of hers. "I wash my hands of her."

"Is that your last word, Mr. Armstrong?" asked the governor.

"It is," said Benjie.

***

Later that evening they were enjoying tea and toast at the forge, telling Richard the story of the afternoon's hearing. Benjie had asked Tom and William to be godfathers to the twins. William said that he was an old man, but Charlie would be an excellent godfather. This meant that Charlie was absolutely full of himself, and nobody could get any sense out of him for a while.

"She might have kept the gang together if she still had the horse," said Benjie, "I wonder what happened to it."

"Hamish said one of his neighbours gained a horse. An old nag turned up in one of his fields, chestnut with a white blaze. Not fit for much but his children make a fuss of it," said Richard.

"Could Martha claim it back?" asked Benjie.

"I think she could if Star had ended up on the English side of the border. But it sounds as if it would be kinder to let him be," said Richard.

"I don't see what is wrong with the poorhouse," said Kit.

"Charlie told us that you both had quite a good time there, but the food was nothing special," said Susan.

"All that bread and water," said Charlie.

"I am not surprised," said Tom.

"I think that the poorhouse has people that Martha does not want to meet, Caleb's mother, for instance. And there may be others that bear a grudge," said William, "It always pays to be nice to people, just in case."

"She tried to kidnap me," said Charlie.

"She tried to get me hung," said Benjie, "accused me of killing Frank to steal the horse. The Coroner didn't put me on trial because I was on my deathbed at the time."

There was a shocked silence as everybody remembered what Martha had said at Frank's inquest. Benjie and Charlie looked at each other. In a way they were proud of their grandmother's strength but neither of them wanted to live with her.

"Tom, I was wondering about what you said at the hearing. What was the risk to my health if I had taken my grandmother back home with me?" asked Benjie.

Tom had been about to say that he thought that Nancy would kill him, but it didn't seem a very good thing to say.

"I don't think Nancy would have been pleased with you," said Tom.

"Has she still got her cane?" asked Sally.

"Not anymore," said Benjie, "I'm not sure where it went."

"I am thinking about what Dr. Jarvis said," said Charlie, "About being nice to people just in case they make trouble for you later."

"You should always be fair and honest in all your dealings," said Richard, "if you upset a customer or a member of your family, it could make a big difference later on. They would never give you the benefit of the doubt because they could never trust you."

"Dr. Jarvis said this morning that my misdeeds would come back to haunt me," said Charlie. Benjie wondered what Charlie had done, but didn't like to ask.

"There is a lesson for all of us there," said Tom, "except for doctors. We usually bury our mistakes."

BIBLIOGRAPHY

The main sources are the 1841 and 1851 England Censuses, for information about work and population movements in the first half of the nineteenth century. The information was supplemented by general reference books: *Our Ancestors Lived* by David Hey, *Albion's People - English Society 1714-1815* by David Rule and *A Social History of England* by Asa Briggs. The internet gave me a vast quantity of information about historical events, court records, working conditions, games and pastimes. I read *A History of Wigton* by T.W. Carrick for the development of a typical small Cumbrian mill town, but the fictitious town is smaller and situated further south. I read Dombey and Son, Mary Barton, Middlemarch and several other early Victorian novels to give me a feel for the social history of the time.

I have used English spelling in deference to Nancy.

Printed in Great Britain
by Amazon